Sweet Corpse of Mine

Cover by Lewellen Designs
Editing by Angie Ramey

SWEET CORPSE OF MINE

Secret Seal Isle
Book 7

LUCY QUINN

1.

OOKIE JAMES PEERED in her closet, wearing only her bra and jeans, looking for something feminine to wear on her date with her boyfriend Dylan Creed. She'd never really been into fashion—that was her best friend Scarlett's territory. And considering she was an ex-FBI-agent-turned-inn-owner, it meant her wardrobe was severely lacking in the flirty department.

She'd shuffled through all her hangers once and was on the second round when she heard the front door open, and Dylan shouted, "Cookie?"

"Upstairs," she called through her open bedroom door.

His heavy footsteps sounded on the stairs below, indicating he was coming up to meet her. "Ack!" She ran back over to her closet and pulled out the first blouse her hand landed on; a white button down shirt, a staple from her FBI days.

At least it hugs my curves, she thought as she shoved her arms into the sleeves and hastily fastened the buttons.

Her fingers were still working the top opening when Dylan appeared in her doorway.

He leaned against the frame, his bright blue eyes sweeping over her. One hand was at his side while the other was hidden behind his back. "Still getting dressed?" he asked, one eyebrow raised.

"Just about done." She adjusted one of the cuffs and moved toward him.

"You really shouldn't have bothered." His eyes gleamed with mischief as he glanced down at her ample cleavage, and his voice lowered as he said, "Could've saved us some time."

She stopped in front of him and placed her hands on his chest, his muscles rippling beneath her touch. "What exactly did you think we were going to do on this date, Mr. Creed?" She glanced at the clock next to her bed. "It's only eleven in the morning."

"I have ideas." He grinned and produced a single yellow rose, revealing what he'd been hiding.

"Oh my," Cookie gushed, taking the flower and burying her nose in the sweet scent. "This smells wonderful." She looked at him over the rose, her eyes meeting his, and added, "Thank you."

"You're welcome." Taking a step forward, he wrapped one arm around her waist and lowered his lips gently to hers.

His kiss was gentle at first as Cookie leaned into him, the floral scent of the rose mixing with his pure male spice. Then he deepened the kiss and gently started walking her back toward the bed.

Cookie pulled back slightly, catching her breath and asked, "Why Mr. Creed, are you trying to seduce me?"

"Is it working?"

Her entire body was heated, and she thought he'd had a point when he said she hadn't needed to bother getting dressed. "Maybe."

"Then let me try harder." He gently took the rose from her and placed it on her nightstand. But before he leaned in for another kiss he asked, "Is Rain here?"

Cookie shook her head, her eyes trained on his lips, dying for another taste. "Nope."

"Is she due back anytime soon?" Dylan ran his fingers over her cheekbone, his touch sending a shiver down her spine.

"No. She's out playing with Winter." Cookie, needing no further encouragement, reached beneath the hem of his Henley shirt and ran her fingers over his eight pack abs, wondering what she'd done to deserve such a fine specimen of a man.

Dylan sucked in a sharp breath and raised his arms, making it easier for her to pull his shirt off.

Cookie took a moment to unabashedly gaze at his impressive torso. If there was such a thing as perfection, she was certain she was staring at it. Her phone rang from its spot in her back pocket.

Dylan groaned.

"Ignore it," Cookie said and grabbed him by the waist of his jeans, pulling him in so close that she felt every inch of him.

"If you insist." He placed a trail of kisses down her neck as he undid the buttons she'd fastened just a few minutes before. When her blouse was open, exposing her white lace bra, he paused to let out a sigh. "No guests today?"

"Two," Cookie said, breathless as she shrugged out of her shirt. "They've gone on a whale watching trip. Won't be back for hours."

"Good." His hands went to the button of her jeans as Cookie's undid his belt buckle.

Their lips met again and Cookie melted, letting herself get completely lost in him until her butt vibrated as a text came in. She groaned, pulling her phone out of her pocket, and it clattered on the nightstand where she tossed it next to the yellow rose without even bothering to look at it.

"Now, where were we?" she asked Dylan, moving in for another kiss.

"Um, Cookie?" he said, his gaze darting to the phone.

"Ignore it," she said again, turning his head gently so he was looking at her instead of the evil electronic device that was seriously blocking her game.

"It's a 911 from your mother." His tone was flat as he took a step back and picked his shirt up off the floor, already starting to pull it over his head.

Cookie grabbed it out of his hands. "Not so fast, Mister. This is Rain we're talking about here. The 911 could just be that she and Winter ran out of ganga and are expecting me to find her stash in her hippy room under the stairs so that I can bring it to her."

Dylan chuckled.

"It's not funny," she said. But she had to admit that even though she pretended her mother's antics irritated her—and when the two of them first moved to the island after years of being apart, they had—lately Cookie found herself amused. The truth was if Cookie and Scarlett managed to have as much fun as Rain and Winter did in their sixties, she'd call it a win. But it still didn't mean she'd bring her mother pot because she was too stoned to drive and pick it up herself. Cookie was still ex-FBI after all.

"It's a little funny," Dylan said, handing her the phone. "But while you're probably right, it's Rain. And that could mean anything from dead bodies to DUIs."

"Oh, for crying out loud. Don't even say that." Cookie grimaced, knowing he was right. Her mother, while sweet and full of heart, was also a complete trouble maker. If she wasn't spiking her brownies with Mary Jane, she was putting on X-rated holiday revues. It was just her way.

With a sigh, Cookie pulled up her mother's number and hit CALL.

"Cookie! Thank God you got my message. We have an emergency," her mother said by way of greeting, her tone hushed. "You have to get over here ASAP."

"What is it this time?" Cookie asked. "Did you two

get caught skinny dipping down at the cove again?" Just last week Rain and Winter had decided to join the Polar Bear Club and had been "practicing" their skinny dipping debut in the freezing Maine waters. They'd made so much noise, shrieking as they froze their butts off, that someone had called Deputy Swan, the one and only law officer on Secret Seal Isle. Rain had been vague on the details, but Cookie had surmised one of the women had flashed Swan a peek at her assets in exchange for letting them off with just a warning.

"Of course not, dear. We planned to do that next week."

"Right." Cookie rolled her eyes and sat on the edge of the bed, pulling Dylan down with her. "So what's the emergency?"

"We found Lydia," her mother whispered into the phone.

"Who's Lydia?" Cookie tried her best to keep the impatience out of her voice, but knew she was losing the battle when Rain spoke again.

"Stop acting like I'm inconveniencing you, Cookie James. This is important."

Cookie sat up straight, this time giving her mother her complete attention. It wasn't often Rain used her "mom" voice, but when she did Cookie could be sure she wasn't crying wolf. "I'm listening."

"Lydia is Blake Rosen's missing wife—you know, Winter's boyfriend."

"Soulmate," Winter said, her faint voice echoing over

the line.

"Right, soulmate," Rain parroted. "He's the love of her life. Don't you remember her telling you she'd marry him in a heartbeat if it weren't for his wife? The one that went missing over five years ago and kept him technically married?"

"Sure, I remember." Not even a week ago, Winter had been mooning about her new boyfriend. They'd been a couple since right after the new year. Cookie hadn't taken her too seriously. In her view, five weeks into a relationship was hardly enough time to know if someone was your soulmate. Cookie had known Dylan for almost a year, and she still didn't have a clue. She loved him, sure. But soulmate? She shook her head. "And now you've found her? Where is she, working at a diner in Hancock and suffering from amnesia?"

Cookie smiled, amused at herself for coming up with a scenario that was even too ridiculous for Rain and Winter.

"Nope. But that would be a far better situation than the one we have on our hands," Rain said in all seriousness.

All humor fled as Cookie narrowed her eyes, staring at Dylan. "Mother, I think you better tell me what's going on."

Her mother sighed into the phone and when she spoke again, her voice was shaky. "We found Lydia in a freezer. She'd dead."

Cookie sucked in a sharp breath. "Whose freezer?

Blake's?" Since over half of all female homicides turned out to be the result of domestic violence, there was a reason the authorities always looked at the spouse first.

"Sort of. I mean, I guess so," Rain hedged.

"Mom, where are you?" Cookie picked up her shirt and started stuffing her arms into the sleeves.

"Sunfish Self Storage down by the ferry terminal."

"Unit number?" Cookie asked as she grabbed Dylan's hand and tugged him off the bed.

"Thirteen."

Of course it was. "We're on our way. Don't touch anything."

2.

EVEN THOUGH THE island was so small everything was basically within walking distance, Cookie asked Dylan to drive her to the self-storage. Besides it being February and bitter cold, she didn't want Rain and Winter to spend any more time than necessary with the body. Knowing them, they'd already unwittingly tampered with the evidence.

Dylan held the door open for Cookie, and she rushed into the small office, eager to get out of the blistering wind. The warmth stung her cheeks as she walked up to the counter and eyed the thin, unkempt man leaning back in his chair with his feet propped up on the desk and crossed at the ankles. A small thirteen-inch television flickered on the wall in front of him.

Cookie cleared her throat.

The man turned his bloodshot, glassy eyes toward her and squinted. "Hey." A sloppy smile claimed his lips as he added, "Aren't you the hottest thing to come through my door since July." The guy chuckled at his own joke.

Dylan coughed, covering his laugh.

Cookie shoved her elbow into his rib, silencing him. "Thanks, I think. I'm actually here to meet someone at their storage unit." Cookie gestured to the glass door to the left that led to the warehouse of units. "Mind if we just slip through?"

The man dropped his feet to the floor and pushed himself up, trying to stand, but he stumbled and grabbed onto the desk to right himself. "Whoa." He laughed. "Guess that weed was stronger than I thought." He took two steps, filling the little office with a crackling sound.

Cookie glanced down and spotted a pile of vending machine snack wrappers. Damn, where had he put it all? He appeared to be just about six feet tall but looked to weigh no more than a hundred and forty pounds. She was willing to bet ten pounds of it was from the junk food he'd just consumed.

She was also willing to bet it was no coincidence that he was higher than a kite since Rain and Winter had just happened to find themselves rummaging around in someone else's storage unit.

"Who are you here to meet?" the guy asked.

"Rain and Winter. Two women I'm betting you know. They need help moving something." It wasn't a total lie. Lydia would have to be moved at some point, but Cookie was hoping the M.E. would take care of that.

"Ah, Rain and Winter." He gave them a conspiratorial grin and an exaggerated wink. "I know all about them. Real cool grandmas. My nana could take a couple lessons from them."

Dylan's body shook with silent laughter, no doubt about the grandma crack. Rain would be mortified if she knew anyone thought she was a day over forty.

"I'm sure they'd love to give her few pointers," Cookie said and tugged Dylan over to the door. "We're kind of in a hurry, so if you wouldn't mind buzzing us through…"

"Right." The man nodded his head a few times then seemed to remember what it was he was supposed to be doing and pressed a button under the counter. A loud buzzer sounded, and Cookie pushed her way through to the stark white hallway with bright orange garage doors.

"That was interesting," Dylan said as he followed Cookie past the first row of storage units.

She let out a *harrumph* and turned right, following the numbers toward unit thirteen.

"Are you sure this is it?" Dylan asked when they got there.

The door was closed, and as far as Cookie could tell the place was deserted. Cookie pressed her ear to the metal door and heard the faint sound of laughter. Good Lord, what were they up to? Considering her mother's grave tone on the phone, whatever Rain and Winter were doing, it couldn't be good. "This is it," Cookie confirmed.

"You're sure?" he asked, his expression skeptical.

"Yep. Go ahead and open it."

Dylan shrugged and reached down, grabbing the metal handle, and the door rattled as it went up with apparent ease. Cookie and Dylan stood there for a moment, their mouths open as they surveyed the scene.

A queen-size bed covered with a royal purple silk bedspread was pushed up against the back wall. A matching shag rug covered the concrete floor, and in the corner next to the bed was a nightstand with a large candle and two empty wineglasses. A floor lamp was set to low, giving the space an intimate feel with romantic lighting.

To the left, there was a sub-zero freezer looking out of place, and standing in front of it were Winter and Rain. Both of them were dressed in pushup corsets, black stockings, and garter belts. To the right was a chest of drawers, the top drawer open with various bras and silk lingerie spilling over the side.

"Well, hello there," Dylan said not even bothering to try not to laugh. "Let me guess, Playboy Bunnies?"

"I am a bunny," Rain said, using both hands to lift her breasts and enhance her cleavage. "Winter is a burlesque dancer." She reached over to her friend's breast and flicked a tassel dangling from it. "You should see what she can do with these."

Cookie's gaze landed on Winter's chest and indeed, she realized, Winter's corset stopped just below her breasts and she was wearing pasties, complete with tassels.

"I think I'm a natural," Winter said and started

gyrating so that her tassels swirled around with vigor.

"Yes!" Rain pumped her fist into the air. "You're getting really good at it. I bet you could get a job with Miss Millie's Maidens over in Hancock. I hear they're always looking for fresh tassel talent."

"I am impressive." Winter stared down at her chest as she increased the speed of her spinning.

"I wonder if I could do that." Rain reached for a pair of tassels sitting on top of the freezer with one hand and started to unlace her corset with the other.

"Mother!" Cookie cried, finally finding her voice. "What in the ever-loving hell are you two doing?"

Rain dropped the pasties and immediately stopped undoing her laces. A look of contrition washed over her as her cheeks flushed. "Nothing."

"It looks like you're trying on another woman's lingerie," Cookie said, peering at her mother's enlarged pupils. It was no surprise to Cookie that her mother, and no doubt Winter, had been getting high before they rummaged through Lydia's intimates, not to mention that would confirm where the storage worker had gotten his stash.

"It's not like she's going to be able to use it again," Winter said in a small voice.

"Right," Rain agreed. "It'd be a shame to let such quality silk go to waste."

A dull ache formed over Cookie's left eye, and she forced herself to remain calm. "You do realize this is a crime scene, right?"

"Yes," Rain said, somewhat defensively, as she turned to point at the freezer. "We didn't touch anything inside there."

Winter turned her attention to the freezer, and Cookie noted the visible shudder that rolled through her mother's dear friend. The older woman wrapped her arms around her body and rubbed her arms as if she were imagining what it would be like to be trapped in the cold.

"At least there's that," Cookie said, shaking her head. She moved in front of the freezer, noting the framed picture of a pretty brunette and dried roses lying in front of it as if it were a gravestone. "Is that Lydia?" Cookie asked Winter.

"Looks like her. I've only seen her in a picture in Blake's study."

Cookie nodded and after pulling her sleeve down to cover her fingers, she reached over and lifted the top of the freezer. Sure enough, a frosty version of a woman with long brunette hair stared back at her with glassy eyes. "Damn," Cookie muttered and let the freezer close with a thud.

"Should I call Swan?" Dylan asked, placing his hand on the small of her back.

"No!" Winter and Rain said at the same time.

Cookie turned and crossed her arms over her chest. As much as she distrusted Swan with anything more serious than a traffic ticket, there were protocols to follow. "I don't think I really have a choice."

SWEET CORPSE OF MINE

"But he's so lazy he'll immediately blame Blake," Winter said. "And I know he didn't do this."

Cookie raised her eyebrows in question. "The husband is the first one the authorities will suspect. And clearly this unit is some sort of love nest." But even as she said the words out loud, her analysis felt off. Why would a woman and her husband use a storage unit for a secret tryst? She supposed it was possible they were role playing and pretending to have an affair to spice things up in the bedroom.

"No," Winter insisted. She reached into the chest of drawers and grabbed a handful of garments. "Blake doesn't even like lingerie. Something about his mom and dad and an ill-timed nooner that he accidently walked in on traumatized him. He said ever since then, every time he sees a silky negligee it kills his mood. He prefers me to go naked." She gave Cookie a self-satisfied smile. "I just strip. Economical when you think about it."

"It so many ways," Rain added.

Cookie's eyes met Dylan's.

He shrugged. "Sounds reasonable."

Cookie had to agree. For once, Winter was making perfect sense.

"I've heard the nooner story, Cookie," her mother said. "It's true. Blake wouldn't be into any of this stuff. Too bad too, because I know Hale would lose his mind if he saw me shake my groove thang in this little number." She wiggled her hips and leered at Dylan. "Wouldn't you like to see Cookie—"

"That's enough of that," Cookie said, holding her hand up. "What Dylan would like to see me in is not up for discussion."

"Sure it is," Dylan muttered.

Rain giggled while Cookie shot him a not-now look. "Listen," she said to Winter. "I tend to agree with your assessment about Blake, but the fact is I don't have a choice here. The local law has to be notified. And unfortunately, that's Swan. But I'll do what I can to make sure the case is thoroughly investigated."

"She'll call Hunter," Rain said with authority.

"I am not going to call Hunter," Cookie insisted. Hadn't she been deputized? She didn't need Hunter. Besides having access to FBI records, he was no more qualified to lead a case than she was. "He doesn't have to handle every investigation here on the island."

"You promise Blake won't be unjustly accused?" Winter asked, wringing her hands.

Cookie knew better than to promise that so she said, "I'll do what I can," and pulled out her phone to make the call.

3.

COOKIE AND DYLAN stood outside the closed storage unit, waiting for Rain and Winter to change out of Lydia's lingerie. It'd been close to ten minutes already, and Cookie's patience was running thin considering she'd already called Deputy Swan and he could arrive any minute.

"Hurry up," she said, pounding a fist on the metal door.

"Just a sec," she heard Winter call. "Your mom's just trying to squeeze back into her leather pants. I think we might need a shoehorn to get them over her backside."

"Hey!" Rain called out, clearly offended.

"Leather pants?" Dylan asked.

Cookie closed her eyes and shook her head. "Mom saw a picture of Hayley Holloway in a pair of skin-tight red leather pants, and all I've heard for the past week is how hot she'd look in them."

"Right." Dylan nodded as if her explanation was perfectly reasonable for a sixty-something-year-old inn keeper. Cookie chuckled, loving the way Dylan just rolled with her mother's shenanigans.

The sound of metal clanging indicated the door was rolling up, and Cookie turned to see her mother in skin-tight red leather pants, black knee-high boots, and white-with-red-hearts cropped T-shirt that appeared to be two sizes too small. A faux fur jacket was slung over her right shoulder.

Cookie blinked as she gazed at what appeared to be an aged rock star stuck in her glory days.

"Someone's ready for Valentine's Day," Dylan said.

"Hale and I have a date later. You like?" She turned around and glanced over her shoulder as if she were posing for a fashion shoot.

Cookie let out a groan but secretly admired her mother's self-confidence, despite the fact her leather pants weren't exactly tight in the rear.

"I think she looks hot," Winter said, defending her friend.

Rain laughed. "I knew my daughter was too uptight for this outfit." She placed a hand on Dylan's arm and waggled her eyebrows at him. "I just hope that for your sake she drops the inhibitions once you're in the bedroom."

Dylan grinned at Cookie, and her face flushed with heat.

"Aha!" Rain's eyes gleamed as she pointed a finger at Cookie. "I knew it! The apple doesn't fall far from the tree after all."

"Mom, do you think we could move on from my love-life and focus on the dead woman in the freezer?" Cookie pressed her fingertips to her temples, hardly believing the words that had just come out of her mouth.

"Of course, Cookie. We can discuss ways to enhance your sex life during dinner," her mother said matter-of-factly as if it were ordinary family meal conversation.

"Oh for crying out—"

"There you are," a male voice said, interrupting Cookie's outrage.

She turned and spotted the doughy, dark-haired deputy working his way toward them. He moved with a lumbering gait, as if he was having trouble putting one foot in front of the other, and his cheeks were rosy. No doubt he'd already been into the sauce. It was a rare occasion when one encountered Deputy Swan sober. It appeared today wasn't going to be one of them.

Another man rounded the corner, his long strides quickly overtaking the deputy. He was tall, with a medium build, and had silver hair.

"Blake!" Winter said, rushing to meet him.

He wrapped an arm around her waist, tucking her in close and bending his head to say something Cookie couldn't hear.

Winter pointed at the storage unit. "She's in there."

Blake's face turned to ash as he slowly worked his way into his wife's love nest. Once he was in the middle of the unit, he stood stock-still, taking in the surroundings. His eyes focused on the bed for a long moment, and then he noticed the still-opened drawer. He sucked in a sharp breath and shook his head in pure disbelief.

He glanced back at Winter, who'd stayed just outside of the unit by Rain's side. "How did you know to come here?" he asked.

Winter visibly swallowed and glanced away before confessing, "I read her journal."

"What?" He turned and walked back to Winter, staring down at her in confusion.

"I... um, the other day when you were in the shower, I was in your study, or I guess the room that used to be Lydia's study. Anyway, I was looking for a piece of paper to write you a note and let you know I had to run an errand. But while I was rummaging around for a pen in the top drawer, a small key that had been taped to the underside of the desk was jarred loose and just plopped down, taunting me."

"So you decided to use it?" Cookie asked before she could stop herself.

Winter grimaced. "I don't know what came over me. The curiosity was overwhelming." She stared into Blake's disbelieving expression. "I was sure the key went to the decorative box on the desk, and I never even stopped to think there might be secrets in there. I just... well, anyway. That's where I found her journal. The last entry was over five years ago and she wrote about the hot... um, her encounters here with her lover." Winter looked at Blake with compassion in her eyes.

"Whoa, nelly, oh boy were they—" Rain stopped herself when Winter and Cookie both glared at her.

Cookie shook her head. Now was so not the time. The man may have just learned his wife had been having an affair and was dead—or that his secret had finally been discovered.

Rain bit down on her lower lip and glanced away, a contrite expression on her face.

"So instead of telling me about it, you and Rain just decided to come here?" Blake asked, disbelief in his tone.

Winter put a soft hand on his chest, staring up at him with tears in her eyes. The woman who'd been trying on negligées and laughing with Rain was long gone, and Cookie was relieved to see her taking this seriously, even if Rain was still bordering on the ridiculous. "I didn't want to upset you if it turned out to be nothing… but then we found her."

"Where is she?" Swan demanded.

"In there, cooling off," Rain said, pointing to the freezer. "She looks great for being dead for five years."

Her mother had a point. Other than being blue and lifeless, the body hadn't deteriorated at all. It would make the forensics much easier to tackle.

Swan stalked over to the freezer and yanked the top open. "Yep. She's a popsicle."

Blake walked up behind him, gasped, and then closed his eyes as his face paled. His body swayed, and Cookie was afraid the man was going to pass out.

"Whoa," Cookie said, moving to stand beside him.

She wrapped her arm around his waist, steadying him. "Are you all right?"

Blake shook his head, his entire body trembling.

"You wouldn't be either if you'd just been caught red-handed," Swan declared, pulling his handcuffs off his belt.

"What?" Cookie, Rain, and Winter all said at the same time.

"It's obvious Blake killed Lydia. Look at how upset he is that his current lover found his wife." He pointed at Blake, who was shivering, making it clear to Cookie that he was in shock. Who wouldn't be after finding out their missing spouse has spent the last five years just a few miles away in a freezer?

"You're going to have to come with me, sir." Swan snapped a cuff onto Blake's right wrist and was reaching for the left when Winter grabbed hold of the deputy and forcibly pulled him away from her man.

"What is the matter with you? He didn't do it," she insisted. "How could he? He didn't even know this place existed?"

"He wants you to think that." Swan grabbed her wrist and removed her hand from his arm. "Now let me go before I take you in for obstruction."

Winter's eyes narrowed and she opened her mouth to protest, but Blake cut her off. "Don't, Winter," he said, his voice low and hoarse. "I don't want you mixed up in this."

"But I'm the one who found her. I'm already in the

middle of it," she insisted.

"Please," he pleaded. "Don't make this worse. I'll go and answer his questions. I'm sure I'll be home in a few hours."

Swan snorted his disbelief.

"This is crazy," Cookie said. "You don't have any evidence."

"I will after we get a confession out of him," Swan said, securing the second cuff around the man's wrist. The deputy yanked Blake out of the storage unit, and with a somewhat steadier step, marched him back toward the office.

"But he doesn't even like lingerie!" Winter yelled after him.

The deputy ignored her, and a moment later they disappeared around the corner.

"No!" Winter buried her face in her hands while Rain rubbed the woman's back in a supportive gesture.

"She told you Swan was a bad call," Rain told Cookie. "Should've called Hunter."

"Even if I had, we still would've had to inform Swan," Cookie said, irritated. What exactly had Swan been thinking? There was less than zero evidence linking Blake to the murder of his wife. At best, Swan had reasons to question the man, but to arrest him? No. He was the laziest excuse for a law enforcement officer Cookie had ever witnessed.

"You have to help him, Cookie," Winter pleaded, tears streaming down her face. "He's innocent. I can feel it in my bones."

"He's really not the murdering type," Rain said. "I can sense these things."

"I'm sure you can," Cookie said absently, staring at the freezer. Swan hadn't searched the unit for clues. He hadn't even called anyone to come get the body. She sighed. Even if Winter hadn't been her mother's closest friend, she already knew she'd get involved. Swan was just too incompetent to handle a potential murder case.

"You're going to need help with this," Dylan said, reading her mind.

She nodded. "I know."

"Your mother's right. You should call Hunter."

Cookie glanced up at him, meeting his deep blue gaze. "Are you okay with that? Having Hunter hanging around again?"

He gave Cookie a half shrug and a cocky smile. "I'm pretty sure that after our date the other night, I don't have much to worry about."

Cookie's mind filled with memories of them locked in her bedroom, and her lips twitched into a smile of her own. "You're right. You don't."

Then she pulled out her phone and dialed.

4.

COOKIE STOOD OUTSIDE of the storage unit building and stared up at the bluebird sky. Water dripped steadily from icicles onto the pavement as the sun offered unseasonable warmth for Maine in February. She knew she was going to have to do some convincing to get Hunter to come to Secret Seal Isle again and opted to make her call away from any prying ears. Dylan's included. Not only was she sure her former FBI partner had used up all his vacation days for the series of murder investigations she'd pulled him into over the past year, she was fairly certain he'd used up most of his favors as well.

Considering Hunter had made it clear he wanted a more physical kind of partnership with Cookie, which she'd certainly considered with painstaking care, and the fact she'd eventually turned him down for Dylan Creed, Cookie was confident getting Hunter back on the island was going to be more than difficult.

She took a deep breath and hit CALL.

Hunter answered on the first ring. "The answer is no, Charlie."

"Well, hello to you, too," Cookie said in a sweet voice even though she was annoyed at his reaction. "The weather here is downright balmy for this time of year. I think we're experiencing the January thaw a little late. How is it in Philly?"

"You called to talk about the weather?" Hunter chuckled. "Whatever it really is, I don't want to hear it."

"Fine," she said while she twirled a lock of her hair around her finger as if he could see her. "Then I suppose a couple drawers full of lingerie, which by the way hug a woman's curves in all the right ways…" She paused for a moment to let the visual secure itself in Hunter's mind. "A secret love nest and a body on ice for five years wouldn't interest you."

"Lingerie that hugs—how would you even—" He let out a huff of annoyance. "No, Charlie. It doesn't. And need I remind you that you're no longer in law enforcement, which makes you a meddling citizen? Stay out of it and let the professionals do their job." The line went dead, and there was no question he'd just hung up on her.

"Hmpf," she said as she stuck her phone back in her pocket, embarrassed to admit to herself that his words stung. She may have given up her FBI badge, but that didn't make her a meddling citizen. She *had* been deputized after all. Besides which, Swan was the only other professional on the island, and that thought made her shudder.

She turned to the sound of the creaking door as Dylan walked out of the storage unit office. Sunlight glistened on his dark hair, turning it a soft brown, as his smile warmed her heart and melted her bad mood away. Normally that would be no small feat, but Cookie was most definitely in love.

Dylan's eyes twinkled with the mischief of earlier in the day when he asked, "Your mother and Winter are busy putting away the… ah, clothing they borrowed for their impromptu fashion show. Are we off the hook until Agent O'Neil shows up?"

Oh boy did Cookie wish that were true, because what had almost happened in her bedroom earlier was preferable to frozen women and—Well, heck. A roll in the hay with Dylan Creed was preferable to everything as far as she was concerned. She let out a sigh. "It looks like I'm on my own with this one. Hunter said no." She didn't bother to mention that Hunter also told her to stay away from the case as well.

Dylan stepped forward and hooked a finger in the opening of her parka to tug her closer. He glanced down her shirt for a moment before meeting her gaze. The grin on his face disappeared, replaced by something more serious, and he said, "Let me know how I can help."

Cookie smiled at him. Dylan Creed was so much more to her than a boyfriend, and she was giddy with the way he was always there for her, no matter what. "Are you sure?"

She thought about all the ways Dylan had been there for her. She knew he was just as capable a partner in an investigation as he was in her personal life, but murder investigations on Secret Seal Isle had a way of turning into more than anyone could ever anticipate. "Think about what you're offering," she said to him.

He smiled down at her. "I'm well aware, Cookie James. Trouble follows you like a seagull after a French fry. You need me."

Cookie lifted up on her tiptoes as she said, "I most certainly do," and she kissed him with the promise of much more.

When she pulled away, Dylan said, "We should get back in there. Rain and Winter were discussing a fundraiser for Blake's legal expenses, and the word burlesque was thrown out."

Cookie groaned and tried to keep the vision of her mother and twirling tassels out of her mind. "Right. And I'll call Jared." As they walked back to the storage units, Cookie called Jared Delgado, the Hancock Medical Examiner, and she braced herself for what she might find when she saw Rain and Winter again.

Fortunately, the two women were still in in their own clothing, and Cookie said to them, "I've called the ME. There's nothing left to do now but wait until he gets here."

"There's something you need to see," Rain said as she held out a piece of jewelry. "Look at this." Cookie took the ornate heart-shaped pendant from Rain and noticed it was actually a locket engraved with *All My Love, D.D.*

"We found it in the drawer when we were putting the lingerie back," Winter said. "I recognize the handiwork. It has to be a piece from Crazy Cari."

"Crazy Cari?" Cookie asked.

"Crazy Cari." Dylan chuckled. "I haven't seen her since the summer she was crowned the final Queen Dumpy. Is she still around?"

"She lives over at the artist colony," Winter said. A good portion of Secret Seal Isle had been designated as an artists-only area decades ago, and a few residents still lived there year round, with many artists visiting every summer.

"Queen Dumpy?" Cookie asked, her brow furrowed in confusion. "Who is this woman? And who would ever want that title?"

"Secret Seal Isle used to have an annual town dump parade where all the residents had to create their costumes from things found at the dump," Winter explained. "The person with the best costume reigned over the parade as Queen or King Dumpy."

"Crazy Cari won almost every year," Dylan said with a chuckle.

"She did win every year. I think that woman trolled the dump on a daily basis to work on her costume." Winter shook her head. "It was a sad day when the department of health stepped in and stopped that tradition."

Cookie frowned wondering why anyone would want

to wear a costume made from items found at the island dump. She decided she was just grateful the ritual had been long discontinued by the time she and Rain had moved to the island, because she'd bet money Rain would have participated.

"The locket's a good clue, Cookie," Rain said. "Right?"

"It is," Cookie admitted. Rain had gotten involved in past investigations, and she had been helpful from time to time. "It's a very good clue, Mom." But her mother's help wasn't something she needed this time, especially since it was Rain's best friend's boyfriend who was under arrest. "We should get you and Winter a ride home," Cookie added, "before Jared gets here."

With her fingers balled up into fists on her hips Rain said, "You're not getting rid of us that easy. We can't just leave Blake in the hands of that pompous, no good, coffee-brandy marinated, over-stuffed shirt of a police officer, Deputy Swan."

Dylan's lips twitched with a smile, but he sobered when he caught Cookie's glare.

"I promise to keep you updated on what I find out," Cookie said. "But you and Winter are too close to this." She softened her voice and reached out to touch Winter's arm. "I don't think Blake killed Lydia either. I'll do my best to get him cleared and find out what really happened. You have my word."

Winter patted Cookie's hand. "Thank you, dear." She glanced around the storage unit and sighed. "Let's call for an Uber."

"When did we get Uber on the island?" Cookie asked, shaking her head. The island was no bigger than a postage stamp. The idea of Uber in their tiny town was ludicrous.

Dylan's lips twitched with amusement as he answered for Rain, "Last week when Stone decided he needed another job so he could by a boat. He wants to start lobstering."

"Stone?" Cookie chuckled. Stone had grown on Cookie since she'd first dealt with him in an accidental death incident. At the time, he had been the local source for illegal marijuana and a bit of an unsavory character, but he wasn't a bad guy. He'd since cleaned up his act, and apparently he now had aspirations for more than basic retail work. Cookie had to give him credit for using legal means to get there.

Rain peered up from her phone. "He's two minutes away. We should get going." As she and Winter left the storage unit, Rain glanced over her shoulder and winked at Dylan and Cookie. "Don't you two do anything I wouldn't do. Actually," She stopped walking and turned to them. "Please do something I would. There's a corset with the—"

"Mother! This is a crime scene."

Rain rolled her eyes at Cookie. "You really do need to loosen up, dear. Am I right, Dylan?"

"Mom," Cookie warned.

Rain tossed her faux fur jacket over her shoulder.

"Fine. Fine. We're going." She turned on her heel and strutted out, thigh-high stiletto boots clicking along the concrete as if she were about to greet her adoring fans.

Dylan's gaze followed her as his whole body shook with silent laughter.

Cookie shook her head. "So just how crazy is this Cari?"

Dylan grinned. "Your mom will like her."

5.

THE OTHER SIDE of the island was far enough away
they could have driven, but since it was such a
beautiful day Cookie and Dylan decided to walk to
Crazy Cari's house instead. Their boots sloshed through
wet snow as Dylan asked, "How do you want to play
this? Good cop, bad cop?"

Cookie chuckled. Dylan had assisted with cases
before, but he excelled at search and rescue, and she'd
never questioned leads with him. Cookie was sure his
idea came from a procedural TV show, but she was
willing to humor him. "Sure," she said. "I'll be the bad
cop."

"Uh-uh, you'd make a terrible bad cop."

"What? I'm the perfect bad cop. What do you think
I do every day with my mother?"

"And yet she still—" Dylan started.

Cookie punched him on the arm. Hard.

"Ouch!"

"You're the one that would make a terrible bad cop,"

Cookie said as Dylan rubbed his well-formed bicep. "You've got every woman in this town swooning over you."

"I do not." Dylan narrowed his eyes at her. "Are you jealous?"

"Darn right I'm jealous," Cookie said. "Far be it for me to stop you, though. They'd all have my head if I nixed their midday, diet-soda-commercial break."

Dylan frowned in confusion as Cookie linked her arm in his and peered up at him with doe eyes. "Oh Dylan, the ice on my roof is so thick I'm afraid of an ice dam. I'd climb up the ladder to get it but—" Cookie batted her eyelashes at him.

Dylan laughed at her. "So you're jealous of Mrs. Dutton, my first grade teacher. She's about seventy-five years old."

"No. She's not the one I'm worried about. It's the women who gathered in the laundromat across the street to watch you when you stripped down from the heat of manual labor." She paused for a moment to recall the image since she was one of those women that day. She remembered thanking the heavens that the inn's washing machine wasn't big enough for the king-size comforters she'd had to launder. "Did you know they have a group text devoted to your whereabouts?"

"They do not!"

Dylan was actually blushing, and Cookie grinned, mostly because she'd made up the part about the group text. She might have also been exaggerating a bit about the laundromat since she'd only overheard two women discussing his assets, but her point was made. "Face it. You're not someone the ladies of this town fear."

"Fine. When we question women, you can be the jealous bid—bad cop." This time Dylan jumped out of the way before Cookie could punch his arm. He pointed off to the right. "That's Crazy Cari's place over there."

Cookie glanced in the direction he indicated to see an old saltbox-style home in disrepair. It was masked by trees and brush, but through the wild landscape she could see bare wood revealed by peeling white paint. Various snow-covered mounds on the front lawn made her suspect more than costume supplies had made their way from the dump to Cari's house over the years.

There was a path in the snow that had been formed by footsteps, and she and Dylan followed it to a breezeway that connected a one-car garage to the house. Cookie pressed the cracked doorbell button, but when they didn't hear it ring, Dylan opened the storm door and knocked on the solid wood door instead.

"Come on in!" They heard a woman call out.

Letting Dylan take the lead since he knew Cari, Cookie held back and followed him in. They were greeted by an array of junk. On the right a narrow passageway to the garage door was bookended by newspapers, yellowed by age and stacked almost to the ceiling. Directly in front of them was a container full of empty cans and bottles as if this were Cari's personal recycling center. To the left was the entry to the house, which was ajar. Dylan poked his head in. "Cari! It's Dylan Creed."

"Hold on a minute," Cari said as Cookie and Dylan stepped into her kitchen. Only it didn't appear to be a place where the woman cooked food. A butcher's block island was set up in the middle of the floor, but instead of a collection of knives or pots and pans hanging overhead it was organized as a jeweler's bench. Cari was blasting a small torch at something that was glowing cherry red and sitting on what looked like a ceramic brick.

The woman turned off the torch and glanced at them with glasses that magnified her eyes to cartoonish proportions. She shoved the glasses up to the top of her head, where gray curls were piled in a haphazard bun. She blew a stray lock of hair out of her face and grinned at them. "I have visitors. How nice to see you again, Dylan."

"Cari," he said, "this is Cookie James. She and her mother bought the old inn."

"Oh. Yes. Lovely place. Brooke was married there in nineteen-something-or-other. I was a bridesmaid." She sighed. "Horrible man. They divorced a few years later. But it was a beautiful wedding." She tilted her head and frowned. "Or was that Stacy? Huh." She walked over to what Cookie suspected was the stove under the visible debris. Cari lifted a cat from one of the burners and dropped him on the floor with a thud. "Can I get anyone some tea?" she asked as she pulled a kettle from behind a precariously stacked pile of dishes on the counter. Dirty or clean, Cookie couldn't tell.

"That won't be—" Cookie began.

Dylan nudged her with his elbow, silently urging her to take the tea.

She gave him an irritated look as if to say she was running this investigation, but when Dylan returned it with a stern one she thought about the fact he knew Cari better than she did. Perhaps it was best if she followed his lead, so she corrected herself. "We'd love some."

"Earl Grey?" A tin appeared from behind a pile of magazines. "Oh! Wait. I just got a lovely blend from Winter Sage's shop. Morning Mellow Mushro—"

"No!" both Dylan and Cookie said in unison. When Cari's eyes widened, Dylan added, "Cookie's allergic to mushrooms. Earl Grey would be perfect for both of us. Thank you."

Cookie poked him in the stomach for throwing her under the bus. She clearly needed to set some ground rules going forward, because this was not how she and Hunter operated. Of course she and Agent O'Neil had been partners for years and were so close they knew what the other was thinking in most situations. For a moment she wished Hunter was there with her for the initial interview instead of Dylan. Having Dylan by her side felt good. Nice. Except he wasn't Hunter, the professional partner she could predict. But if she remembered correctly, she and Hunter had gotten off to a rocky start too.

"Speaking of Winter," she said, "that's why we're here. She thought you might be able to help us with something." Cookie reached in her pocket and pulled out her deputy badge to show Cari. "Dylan and I are investigating the death of Lydia Rosen."

"Lydia!" A light bulb may have gone off in Cari's head because she held up a finger and said, "Maybe it was her wedding...." She shook her head. "No, wasn't her either."

Cookie held back the urge to sigh with her annoyance at the woman's flakiness. But she knew from experience people dealt with the news of death in many ways. She pulled out the heart-shaped locket Rain had found in the lingerie drawer at the storage unit and held it up. "Do you recognize this?"

Cari reached for the pendant, and she smiled as she held it in her palm and stroked the top with her thumb. "Goodness, that certainly is one of my babies."

"We were wondering if you could tell us who you sold it to," Dylan said.

"I couldn't possibly say. I've made dozens like it." She frowned. "Lydia Rosen...huh." Cari glanced up at the ceiling as if she were calling upon magical spirits to help. "Lydia..."

Cookie cleared her throat to bring Cari back to earth, and when the woman looked at her she said, "There's an inscription on the back. Perhaps that will help jog your memory."

Cari returned her glasses to her nose and peered at

the back of the locket. "Hmmm, I engrave a lot of these. D.D." She glanced up at them. "I have no idea who that could be. Hearts are rather popular with men for gift giving." She scanned Dylan with her gaze. "Do you have anyone special you'll need to treat on Valentine's Day, Dylan? I'm sure I could make you something she'd love."

"Well—" he began.

"You must keep sales records," Cookie interrupted. She wasn't ready to hear his answer. Dylan and she were too new for her to begin to think about him giving her jewelry. Or not. Especially engraved heart lockets promising love forever. "Could you check them for us?"

Dylan gave her a sideways glance with an expression Cookie couldn't read. She wasn't sure if it was gratitude for changing the subject or if it was because she was being skittish. The truth was she wasn't sure why she was afraid of his answer.

The teakettle began to scream and Cari went to the stove to prepare the hot drinks. Steam curled up from the cups as the woman brought them over and set them on the small table off to the side of the kitchen. Cookie moved empty shipping boxes off a chair and sat as she said, "So about those records. Do you think you could check them to see if you can find out anything about who might've purchased the locket? It would have been at least five years ago."

"Sure." Cari didn't bother to sit down but instead moved toward the cabinets. She opened one near the sink that Cookie would have used for drinking glasses and then pulled out a shoebox full of what appeared to be receipts. Judging by the haphazard way they were stuffed in the box, Cookie assumed they weren't in any particular order. She glanced at Dylan, who shrugged and then made a show of rolling up his sleeves.

He winked at Cookie and said, "Bring that right over here, Cari, and let's take a look."

Cookie had to give him credit. Dylan was definitely one to dig right into whatever task was presented to him. She pushed her irritation aside to work along with him and Cari as they all began to review the sales slips.

Paper rustled as they pulled out receipts. The cryptic notes caused a headache to throb behind Cookie's eyes, and it was compounded by Cari reminiscing about each piece she'd made. After they had read through everything, it was clear that Cari had either lost the sales slip or had never written anything down pertaining to the locket in question. D.D. would remain a mystery until another day.

Cookie took a sip of her tea to find it was cold. Just like the lead. They'd hit a dead end, and it was time to head home.

6.

COOKIE WAS TIRED, hungry, and cranky. The sun had set and the walk back to the Dylan's truck at the storage facility was cold. And because the melted snow had refrozen and turned the wet streets into slick ice and hard snow, she had to concentrate on her steps to avoid falling. Dylan holding her close was helping, though. He had a way of warming her up that had little to do with the ambient temperature.

"That was disappointing," he said.

"Yeah." Cookie sighed. "It goes like that sometimes. We've still got plenty to go on, so we'll pick up where we left off tomorrow."

They'd reached Dylan's truck and after they climbed in for the short drive he asked, "What's up first?"

"The ME. Jared should have enough information for us to plan how to move forward."

"Perhaps right now we should pick up where we left off much earlier today."

Cookie smiled up at him and noticed the way the

dashboard lighting twinkled in his eyes. Taking him up to her bedroom was a very enticing idea. Although the inn wasn't empty the way it had been that morning.

Dylan pulled in and parked in front of the inn. She said, "We'd have to be quiet. There are guests."

Once he turned off the engine they got out, and he stopped Cookie to turn her to face him. He leaned in close and tipped her chin up with a warm finger. He whispered, "I'm not the one that needs reminding."

Heat rose so fast to Cookie's cheeks she was afraid they were steaming. "I—"

Dylan said, "You're so sexy when you blush." Before Cookie could give Dylan a snappy comeback he kissed her. Suddenly her cheeks weren't the only thing steaming, and she thought she might not have to worry about throwing down rock salt on the icy steps in the morning as she began to melt—until they heard the wail of two women crying.

Cookie and Dylan quickly pulled apart.

"Rain," Dylan said.

"And Winter," Cookie added. They gave each other a wry smile and went inside.

Cookie stood just inside the living room, surprised to see Rain and Winter on the couch in front of the television. A movie was playing and the women had a bottle of wine and a box of tissues between them. Cookie frowned. Rain wasn't a big drinker, preferring to get high instead. "Mom?" she asked.

Her mother took a swig from the bottle and sniffed

as she turned to her daughter, tears streaming down her face. "He wants to take her to Paris, but she doesn't want to go."

"Blake?" Dylan asked.

"No," Winter cried. "Preppy. She's dying and he—" she broke into a sob.

Recognizing the film Rain and Winter were watching, Cookie turned to Dylan. "They're talking about the movie." She walked over and grabbed the wine from Rain's hand. "Mom, you know too much alcohol just makes you weepy." She jostled the bottle and the contents sloshed inside letting her know not much was left. "Besides which, *Love Story*? That one makes you cry when you're sober."

Rain nodded. "Pot was making us depressed, so I thought maybe we should change our approach."

Winter lunged over the back of the couch and latched onto Cookie's shirt, making her stumble back. "We have to save Blake, Cookie! What if I never go to Paris?"

Dylan steadied Cookie and intervened to peel Winter off of her. Winter's rings clattered against the wine bottle as she snatched it out of Cookie's hand, and Dylan set the distraught woman back down on the couch as he said, "It's going to be okay. We'll get Blake cleared as soon as we can."

She clutched the bottle of wine to her chest dramatically. "Then where is he? He's in that—" She couldn't finish her sentence as she broke out into fresh tears.

Dylan patted her back, trying to comfort the woman. "These things take time, Winter. You have to be patient."

Winter let out a hiccup before lifting the wine and guzzling down the remains of the bottle. Then she cuddled up to Rain, who hugged her friend tight.

"I'll take you to Paris, honey." A bit of the usual Rain peeked through when she turned and winked at Cookie. "Those Parisian men won't know what hit them."

Dylan leaned down and whispered in Cookie's ear. "Perhaps we should leave them to their movie."

Cookie nodded as she took his hand and led him into the kitchen. "Would you like something to eat? I'm sure Rain still has some leftover macaroni and cheese. And it doesn't have any medicinal value."

Dylan chuckled. "That would be nice. Thanks."

Cookie popped the casserole into the microwave and pushed a few buttons. It beeped and then began to whirr as Cookie said, "So tomorrow. First we'll go to the ME and see if he's determined the cause of death. And then—"

"Do you have a red dress?" interrupted Dylan as if she hadn't been talking.

"What?"

"A red dress. Do you own one?"

"Uh." Cookie frowned as she tried to figure out why he wanted to know. "Yes. I do."

Dylan gave her a sly smile. "Good."

"Ooookay," she drew out. "About tomorrow. After the ME we should probably go back to the storage unit and see if—"

"Heels. The ones that are tall and skinny. What do they call those?"

"Stilettos," Cookie said.

"That's right. Do you own any of those?" he asked. "Preferably black."

Dylan was up to something, and Cookie smiled to herself as she walked over to grab two dishes from the cabinet. "I do." She couldn't resist teasing him so she continued with the investigation conversation as she spooned out pasta onto the plates. "We should get our hands on the surveillance tapes from the storage facility."

Cookie took the food over to the kitchen table and handed a dish to Dylan.

Yes," he said. "We should definitely do things with our *hands*." He scooped up some macaroni with his fork and lifted it up to let it hover in by his lips. "And our mouths."

Cookie grinned at him. "I don't think you're talking about the investigation, Dylan Creed."

He raised his eyebrows. "Very perceptive, Detective." Reaching over, he took her hand in his. "Would you have dinner with me on Valentine's Day?"

"Hmm." Cookie resisted the urge to scream with excitement like a teenager and throw herself at him as if he'd asked her to the prom. Instead, she tilted her head to the side and pretended she was considering his proposal. "Do you own a crisp white dress shirt? The kind that requires cufflinks?"

Dylan's eyes twinkled with the kind of amusement that said he was enjoying this game too. "I do."

"Necktie? Preferably something red. To match my dress." She shook her head. "No. It should be blue. To match your eyes."

Dylan's voiced deepened as he leaned closer to her. "I can rustle something up."

Cookie leaned in too so that their mouths were only inches apart. "Good. Now about the pants." She glanced down at his plump lower lip as her voice got husky. "They should be snug but not too tight in the rear."

"Yeah," Dylan breathed as he pressed his nose against hers.

Cookie let out a small moan before she said, "Then the answer is yes."

7.

D YLAN WRAPPED HIS arm around Cookie's waist and pulled her in close as they walked toward the double doors of the ME's office. They were in the basement of the sheriff's building on the mainland in Hancock on their way to pump the medical examiner, Jared Delgado, for information. After a large pancake brunch, courtesy of Rain, she and Dylan had hopped the ferry, hoping this visit would be more fruitful for the investigation than the one they'd paid to Crazy Cari.

Cookie smiled up at Dylan, and even though her initial instinct was to pull away, to keep everything as professional as possible while dealing with the ME, his warmth was so welcoming she leaned into him, unable to help herself.

They were still holding on to each other when they walked through the doors.

"Well, isn't that sweet." The gruff sarcastic voice cut through Cookie with a swiftness that made her jump out of Dylan's embrace.

"Hunter?" Cookie asked, her hands on her hips as she gaped at her former FBI partner. The tall, dark-skinned man was dressed impeccably, as always, in a dark gray suit and was as handsome as ever. Only instead of the welcoming grin he usually gave her, he was barely hiding a scowl. "What are you doing here?"

"Apparently I'm investigating a murder." He ignored Dylan as he answered her in a clipped tone.

"I thought you said you weren't interested?" Cookie challenged, completely annoyed she'd been blindsided.

"Turns out Sheriff Watkins didn't trust the local law with such a high profile case. She called and asked for me specifically." His expression was smug as he cast a dismissive glance in Dylan's direction.

Cookie curled her hands into fists and took in a deep breath, trying to control the anger welling deep inside her. He hadn't known she was on her way to see Jared. What had he thought? That he'd interview the ME without her? That wasn't how their partnership worked… at least not in the past. And it sure as heck wasn't going to work that way now. "You didn't think maybe you should call and let me know you were on your way?"

Hunter shrugged. "Why? I've got this. It is my job. Whereas, last I checked, you have an inn to run."

Ouch. That was harsh. If Cookie hadn't been so angry with him, she'd have been hurt. "You of all people should know I'm not going to let this case go. I promised my mom and Winter I'd get to the bottom of this."

"Precisely why you shouldn't get involved." Hunter crossed his arms over his chest. "Conflict of interest."

Cookie snorted. She'd spoken to Sherriff Watkins the night before and gotten the go ahead to work the case. Watkins had mentioned she'd assign the case to an active investigator for the chain of command, she just hadn't mentioned that might be Hunter. "Please. I never even met the man before yesterday. You're reaching, Hunter."

His unreadable gaze shifted to Dylan, though it was clear his next words were intended for her. "Just giving you an out, since it appears you've been busy."

Dylan cleared his throat as if he was going to respond, but Cookie placed a light hand on his arm, silently asking him to let her handle this.

"I don't need an out," Cookie said and turned her attention to the two people staring at them from the desk. A petite woman with curly black hair was perched on top of the desk. She wore black skinny jeans, a form-fitting *Science Girl* T-shirt and knee-high, lace-up boots. In contrast, the lanky Hancock ME had on beige Dockers and a blue and white striped button down shirt. His white lab coat completed the look. "Jared, Frankie. It's good to see you both."

"You, too, Cookie," Frankie, Jared's hot-nerd girlfriend, said with a grin. She swept her gaze from Hunter to Dylan and back to Cookie. "Looks like you've got your hands full."

Cookie chuckled and arched one brow as she stared

pointedly at the items scattered over Jared's desk. "I could say the same for you."

Frankie grinned. "We're working out our Valentine's Day plans. What do you think?" She grabbed two pairs of underwear that were scattered on the desk and held them up. One was black and red with laces on the sides, and the other was pure black with a lacy overlay. "Latex or silk?"

"Silk," Hunter said just as Dylan said, "Latex."

Cookie gasped which she quickly hid with a cough. Had she heard that right?

"Reeeeally," Frankie drew out the word, her smile turning to a mischievous grin as she eyed Dylan. "Not what I expected."

"Me neither," Cookie mumbled.

Frankie held up the black and red shiny latex underwear for Jared's approval. "What do you think, Jared? Want to try these? The laces make them somewhat adjustable. I bet they'd fit you well enough."

Dylan couldn't hold back a laugh, while Hunter discreetly coughed. Cookie just stood there, staring at them, wide-eyed.

Jared's pale face turned bright red as he stammered, "Frankie, do you think we could talk about this later… when we don't have an audience?"

"It's just Cookie and her two hot men," Frankie said, waving an unconcerned hand. "I mean, who hasn't dressed up a little in order to spice things up in the bedroom? A little latex never hurt anyone… much.

Right, Cookie?"

"Um, what?" Cookie asked, her cheeks going just as red at Jared's. "I'm just here to find out a cause of death. I'm not really the person to ask when it comes to… latex."

"Sounds like Dylan might be the one to ask about that," Hunter said, stepping up beside Cookie. He draped a friendly arm over Cookie's shoulders just like he would've in the old days when they'd been partners. "Cookie here is a little more *traditional*."

Dylan's gaze narrowed in on Hunter's hand now gripping Cookie's shoulder, and his expression tightened with irritation. But instead of taking the bait, he just said, "Do whatever you're comfortable with, Jared."

Cookie, feeling like she was a piece of meat caught between two hungry dogs, shrugged off Hunter's arm and moved to stand next to Jared. He apparently was the only sane person in the morgue at the moment. She cleared her throat. "So, Jared, have you had a chance to examine Lydia yet?"

"Yes." Letting out a sigh of relief, the ME gave Cookie a grateful smile, no doubt just as ready to ditch the underwear conversation as she was. He adjusted his glasses as he stood and walked over to a file cabinet. After producing a file, he flipped it open. "This one is fairly straightforward. Crushed windpipe, cracked vertebrae C2 at the base of the spine. The cause of death is strangulation."

"Any DNA evidence?" Cookie asked.

Jared shook his head. "Not yet. The body is still frozen. We need to slowly let it defrost otherwise the tissue will breakdown and all DNA will be lost. I need about a week."

"If the body is still frozen, how did you determine there's a crushed windpipe and broken vertebrae?" Hunter asked.

Jared waved a hand at a door on the other side of the room. "X-ray. That's all we have for now. I can give you a call after we run any DNA we find."

"Okay," Cookie said, blowing out a breath. "It's a start."

Hunter pulled a small notebook from his pocket and tapped his pen on the cover. "Crime of passion."

"That seemed fairly obvious yesterday," Dylan said.

Hunter narrowed his eyes at the other man then cut his gaze to Cookie. She could tell by his pinched expression he wasn't at all happy Dylan knew more than he did about the case. Well, that was just too bad, wasn't it? She'd called him yesterday, and he hadn't wanted any part of the case then. She wondered what Watkins had said to convince him to come to Secret Seal Isle. Because after he'd hung up on her, she was certain she wasn't going to see him any time soon.

"Yeah. Who would've ever thought to have a love nest at the island storage warehouse?" Jared shook his head and grimaced. "Can you imagine dropping off your grandmother's old furniture and hearing what must've been going on in there?"

"Sheet metal walls don't provide much of a sound barrier," Dylan agreed.

"We should probably talk to the people who rent the neighboring units, see if they know anything," Hunter said.

We? Cookie thought. Was Hunter including Dylan in that equation? He'd helped them solve cases before, but now that she was officially dating Dylan, the three of them working together would definitely be a crowd. "It's been five years. I don't know how much luck we'll have talking to the other renters, but it's worth a shot I guess."

"I guess it's a plan, then." Hunter thanked Jared and nodded to Frankie. "Hope Valentine's Day works out."

Jared's face flushed again as he nodded and averted his gaze.

"Yeah, man." Dylan clasped Jared on the shoulder. "Just remember not to wear them for too long. You don't want to experience any chaffing."

A vision of Dylan wearing nothing but latex boy shorts flashed in her head and she couldn't help the chuckle that bubbled up from the back of her throat.

"Don't you worry about that," Frankie said with a wink. "I'm not that patient."

Dylan just smiled and held his hand out to Cookie.

Swallowing her laughter, Cookie slipped her hand into his, told Jared she looked forward to hearing from him once he had the DNA results, and then waved at Frankie as they followed Hunter out of the morgue.

Once they were out on the street, Hunter stopped,

took one look at Cookie and Dylan's joined hands, and tightened his jaw. "I guess our first stop is the storage place."

Uncomfortable with the PDA in front of Hunter, Cookie gently pulled her hand from Dylan's and stuffed both into her jacket pockets. "Seems like the logical first step. We can also find out who's been paying the rent for the last five years."

"And check out security tapes to see who's been to the unit recently," Dylan added.

"Okay." Hunter stared over Cookie's shoulder, his gaze fixed on the churning bay behind her. "I've got the Mustang, so I'll meet you there." Without waiting for a response, he strode off, his shoulders hunched and his head down.

"I guess that means we're walking?" Dylan asked her.

She nodded. "Looks like it." Putting Hunter out of her mind for the moment, she slipped her hand into his jacket pocket, twined her fingers through his and said, "Come on, Mr. Creed. There's a boat we need to catch."

He smiled down at her. "But first we stop in for hot cocoa."

"You really know the way into a girl's heart," Cookie said, letting him lead her to a café across the street.

"No," he said, opening the door for her. "I know the way into *my* girl's heart."

8.

THE DAY WAS crisp and clear with the sun shimmering off the water. The sea salt scented the air, and if it hadn't been for the biting wind chilling her to the bone, Cookie would've gladly stayed near the railing of the ferry. But when she shivered, Dylan tugged her into the cabin. It was late morning and the ferry was almost empty.

Empty except for the three cars parked down below, one of them Hunter's black Mustang rental. She knew if Dylan hadn't been there with her, he would've joined her upstairs and spent the ride brainstorming theories and leads to pursue. They'd banter like they always had and fall into the all too familiar pattern they'd long ago established as partners. A pang of loss made her feel as if a piece of her had been taken and there was nothing she could do about it.

She'd chosen Dylan at Christmas, and she had to learn to live with the consequences of her decision.

"You okay?" Dylan asked, peering at her.

She forced a smile. "Sure. Just thinking about the case."

"More like the FBI agent sulking in his rental," he said, not unkindly, as he waved toward the cars below.

"No. I wasn't. I…" Cookie sighed. "You're right. I just don't want things to be awkward. Why can't we just go back to the way it used to be?"

Dylan shook his head. "You don't really believe that's possible, do you? They man asked you to move back to Philly with him not too long ago. You not only turned him down, but you chose someone else instead of him. A guy doesn't get over that sort of thing easily. Give him some time. Once he's made peace with it, I'm sure he'll come around."

Cookie stared up at him in awe. "How did you, a former Navy Seal, get to be so insightful?"

He winked. "I've always been an old soul."

Even though he said the words as if he was joking, Cookie knew he was right. Part of the reason she was drawn to him was his calm, steady nature. It certainly didn't hurt that he was hot and a really good sport when it came to her mother's shenanigans. But his quiet, solid nature calmed her, made her feel at peace, made her feel at home. She leaned into him, grateful he wasn't threatened by her former partner, and rested her head on his shoulder. "You're pretty great, you know?"

He kissed the top of her head. "Right back atcha, Ms. James."

COOKIE LEAD THE way up the hill from the ferry and spotted Hunter's Mustang parked near the entrance of Sunfish Self Storage. Hunter was leaning against the car, his arms crossed over his chest as he waited for them.

"Have a nice ferry ride?" Cookie asked, stopping in front of him.

"I enjoyed the quiet and took some notes."

"On?"

"The case," he said as he turned, reaching for the door. "Ready to start asking some questions?"

Cookie blew out an irritated huff. "Want to fill me in on your notes first?"

Hunter sighed. "Come on, Charlie. Are we really going to do this now? I was doing what I always do—coming up with theories so I know what to ask."

"Right. Something we always did together." Cookie swept past him, afraid if she continued the conversation she'd say something she'd regret. "Let's just do this."

"I couldn't agree more," Hunter mumbled and followed her and Dylan inside.

The manager, dressed in a stained T-shirt and grimy jeans, was just as unkempt as he had been the day before. Only this time his eyes weren't bloodshot and there weren't snack wrappers all over the floor. Instead, he had a large coffee mug on his desk and an overflowing ashtray. The stench of cigarettes and body odor permeated the air.

Cookie took a few steps back from the desk and made a conscious effort to breathe through her mouth.

Hunter, however, apparently was missing his olfactory senses, because he leaned an elbow on the counter and said, "Good morning."

"You need to rent a unit?" the man asked, barely glancing at Hunter.

"No, but I do have some questions about Lydia Rosen and what you might know about that situation."

The man stood up and walked over to the counter. His disinterested gaze swept over Hunter, then Dylan, and finally landed on Cookie. His eyes lit up and a greedy smile claimed his lips. "You again. You're Cookie, right? Rain's daughter."

"I am," Cookie said, stepping up beside Hunter. "And your name is?"

"Isaac." He squinted as he studied her.

"Nice to see you again, Isaac. As Agent O'Neill already explained, we're here to ask you some questions about Lydia Rosen and the storage locker where her body was found. Can you tell us who paid the rent these last five years?"

"Probably. Do you have something for me? A package from Rain perhaps?"

Cookie rolled her eyes. No doubt he was expecting payment after Rain and Winter bribed him the day before. "No. Like Agent O'Neill said, we're just here to ask some questions."

"That's disappointing." His shoulders slumped as he retreated back to his chair and kicked his feet up on the edge of the desk. "I don't know anything."

"You seemed to think you did when you thought you might be getting high," Cookie said, not bothering to hide the irritation in her tone.

"Hey, those are your words, not mine." He strummed his fingers on the desk and smirked.

"Listen, Isaac," Hunter said, his voice as hard as steel. "You're going to turn on that dinosaur of a computer, give us the name of the person who rented that locker, and then you're going to hand over any security tapes the facility keeps. And you're going to do it without complaint. Got it?"

"What if I don't?" Isaac asked, glaring at Hunter. "You got a warrant or something?"

"No, but if you don't comply, I'm going to arrest you on charges of drug solicitation. And just in time for Valentine's Day. I'm sure you'll find a nice date in the county jail."

Isaac's face turned to ash and he quickly stood, shaking his head. "I was just joking around, man. No need to get all anal agent on me." Instead of firing up the circa nineteen ninety-eight computer, he pulled out a log book and flipped it open. He ran his finger down the page and stopped at number thirteen. "The unit rented to a Blake Rosen. It says paid cash for the entire year."

"Blake?" Cookie blurted. That was Lydia's husband and Winter's boyfriend. "Are you sure?"

He raised his hands up in a surrender motion. "That's what it says. Look for yourself."

Hunter leaned over the counter and eyed the book. He gave Cookie a quick nod.

"Crap," Cookie muttered.

"That's pretty damning evidence against Blake," Dylan said from behind them.

Hunter turned and nodded. "If he's been paying the rent on the unit for the last five years it's going to be easy for a DA to point the finger right at him."

"But why would a married couple rent a storage unit for a love nest?" Cookie asked.

"To spice things up?" Isaac said, pumping his eyebrows. "Keep things interesting? You know it's always the nice respectable ones who are the dirtiest in the bedroom."

"I bet they were the latex type," Hunter said, giving Dylan the side-eye.

Dylan just laughed. "From what we saw, it looked like they didn't have a problem with silk either."

Isaac furrowed his brow. "I feel like I missed something."

"Never mind," Cookie said, shaking her head. "If the storage was paid in cash, it's possible Blake wasn't the one who was actually renting the unit. Cash customers could use any name, right? Do you ask for ID when setting up a rental?"

Isaac shrugged. "Depends. Sometimes. But things are pretty relaxed here. Cash customers don't get hassled too much."

Hunter made another note in his notebook.

"So what you're saying is that it's entirely possible anyone could've rented that unit," Cookie confirmed.

"Sure. I guess."

Cookie pulled out her phone, searched for Winter's profile on Facebook, and tapped on a picture of her and Blake. Then she turned it around and showed it to Isaac. "Do you recognize this man?"

"Yes." Isaac sounded annoyed now. "Of course I do. He was here yesterday. He's the dead lady's husband."

Cookie fought the urge to snap at him. "I meant have you seen him around here before yesterday? Is he the one who paid for the unit?"

"Can't say. I haven't been working here that long." He glanced down at the log. "The last payment on the unit was made ten months ago. I've only been working here since October after old man Pickering died last year, and his son who lives down south inherited the place."

"Figures," Cookie said as she and Hunter shared a resigned glance. More often than not, that was the way investigations went down. Something that should be an easy lead went absolutely nowhere.

"Do you have security tapes?" Hunter asked.

"Yes. It's for our clients' safety." Isaac puffed his chest out as if this were the one thing that mattered. Cookie found it curious he was willing to rent units without ID and let two older women into the storage facility as long as they bribed him with weed, but he was proud that they kept surveillance. If anything, she'd suspected that maybe he'd be less than thrilled about having his actions on tape.

"We're going to need everything you have going back at least five years," Hunter said. "And the names and numbers of the renters of units twelve and fourteen."

"I can't give you the names," he said, crossing his arms over his chest. "Privacy laws."

"If you force me to get a warrant, I don't think this is going to go well for you, Isaac," Hunter threatened. "Not unless you want all of your activities here thoroughly investigated."

Cookie wasn't at all sure there were enough grounds for a warrant, but she was lightly amused at the panicked look on Isaac's face and his immediate change in attitude. "There's no need for that. Jeez. I was just trying to do the right thing." He opened his log book again, scribbled down a couple of names, then returned to the old computer.

The sound of the wall clock ticking filled the silence as they stood around waiting for the computer to transfer files. Cookie's feet began to ache from standing on the cement floor and she leaned over the counter, just to take a break.

Isaac's gaze landed on her, then dropped down as he ogled her.

Cookie glanced down to see her ample cleavage spilling out of her T-shirt. *Son of a…*

"Keep your eyes on your own paper, Isaac," Dylan all but growled as Cookie quickly stood up and tugged at her shirt.

"Hey man, she's the one who put them right in my face."

"He has a point," Hunter said.

Cookie scowled at both of them as she crossed her arms over her chest as if she could retroactively cover herself.

Dylan draped his arm around her shoulders and pulled her to his side protectively.

Finally, the computer dinged and Isaac produced a thumb drive. "It's only thirty days. We don't keep footage for longer than that."

Cookie had expected to learn as much. Most places didn't want to maintain too much data storage.

Hunter took the drive from Isaac then handed it to Dylan. "You should probably handle this. I bet you're the type that likes to watch."

Unfazed, Dylan stuffed the drive into his front pocket and said, "Sure, I can check the footage, but I'm more of a hands-on kind of guy." A self-satisfied smile tugged at his lips as he ran a hand down Cookie's back, stopping only when he reached her hip. "Right, Cookie?"

"Um..." Cookie's face heated at his innuendo and she had to fight to keep from fanning herself.

Hunter's expression darkened as he met her eyes. Then he barked, "Just watch the footage and report back what you find out about the unit and the ones next to it."

"I've got it covered," Dylan said as Hunter strode out the door.

"I think that guy needs to get laid," Isaac said as he flopped back down into his chair.

Dylan opened his mouth to respond, but Cookie held up a hand. "Don't say a word."

Dylan grinned.

"Thank you, Isaac," she said. "Your cooperation is appreciated."

"Sure. Tell Rain and Winter to stop back in sometime. I could really use another… visit." He mimed taking a hit of a joint. "Get it?"

Cookie gave him a flat stare.

Dylan chuckled and shook his head. "I think any idiot would've gotten that." He walked over to the door and held it open for her. "Come on, boss. The investigation awaits."

And one pissed off FBI agent, Cookie thought. Well, what did she expect? For the two of them to be besties? If she was lucky, the most she could hope for was a little cooperation.

When they got outside, Cookie started to shiver. The temperature had dropped at least ten degrees, and the wind had picked up. She quickly zipped up her jacket and jammed her hands into her pockets.

Hunter was standing next to the Mustang, and he opened the passenger door. "Want a ride?" he asked Cookie. "Sorry, Dylan. The back seat is taken up by luggage and files. I guess you'll have to walk back."

She glanced first at Dylan then back to Hunter. "I don't think—"

"Go on," Dylan said, cutting her off. "It's freezing out here, and I'm going to head home anyway."

"Are you sure?" she asked him.

"Positive." After giving her a kiss on the top of her head, he gently nudged her toward the car.

"Okay. Call me later."

He nodded, waved, and strode off in the direction of his island home.

Cookie gratefully climbed into the car, and as Hunter was making his way back around to the driver's seat, she glanced back to see just how much luggage he'd brought.

There was one duffle and nothing else.

Hunter slid into the driver's seat and cranked the engine.

"No room in the back seat?" Cookie challenged.

Hunter gave her a smug smile, stepped on the gas, and tore out of the parking lot.

9.

H UNTER PARKED THE Mustang in front of the inn and turned to Cookie. "Listen, Charlie. I know it was a dick move not giving Dylan a ride, but—"

"Forget it, Hunter," Cookie said, tired of the drama. "He's fine. I'm fine. Let's just get inside where it's warm. I'm sure Rain has something cooking for lunch and we can regroup."

He nodded once and reached for his one duffle bag.

If Cookie hadn't been so annoyed by his childish behavior, she would've laughed. Instead, she jumped out of the car and headed toward the big Victorian over-looking the coastal Maine waters. On warmer days the large porch, complete with wooden swing, was a welcoming refuge. But on days like today, all she wanted was to get inside and tuck away a bowl of Rain's fabulous soup.

With any luck her mother would have some shortbread cookies ready to go too. After the morning out, she could use a little pick-me-up.

She pushed the door open and was greeted by music so loud it was making the walls vibrate. She paused, listening to the words—Prince, and he was singing Purple Rain, one of her mother's favorites. Cookie frowned, fearing the noise would bother their guests, and followed the sound into the living room.

"Mother!" she called but came up short when she spotted Rain in the middle of the room in six inch platforms and a sparkling purple-sequined jacket. Winter was perched on the edge of the couch, her arms in the air as she hooted and catcalled at Rain, who was lip syncing into a large purple mic.

No. Not a mic. A large purple dildo.

"That's impressive," Hunter said into Cookie's ear.

Cookie jumped and closed her eyes, hoping when she opened them she would not see her mother's lips right at the tip of a fake silicone penis.

No such luck.

Taking a deep breath, Cookie walked calmly over to her mother's iPhone doc and pulled the plug. The music stopped, but Rain's voice filled the room as she sang about being a weekend lover.

Oh hell, Cookie thought, trying to force image after inappropriate image out of her mind. Behind her, Hunter was chuckling. She ignored him.

"Cookie," her mother said, still holding the dildo. "What did you do that for? I wasn't finished yet."

"Mother, could you put that *thing* away?" Cookie pointed to her mother's impromptu mic.

"This?" Rain waved the toy in the air. "Why? It's the perfect prop, don't you think?" Her mother grinned at Winter, and the pair of them burst into a fit of giggles.

Cookie did her best to ignore the thing her mother was now pointing at her. "Where are the guests?"

Rain shrugged. "Out to lunch, I think. They'll be back for afternoon tea. Why?"

"Why?" Cookie echoed. "Because perhaps it wouldn't be a good idea for them to walk in on this X-rated revue."

"Oh, Cookie. You're so uptight. I was just trying to cheer up Winter. It's been a rough few days for her." Rain tossed the dildo onto the chair and peered past her daughter. "Hunter? I didn't know you were in town."

"Rain. Winter." He nodded at the two women. "It's good to see you again."

Rain frowned. "Are you staying here?"

"Of course he is, Mom," Cookie said. "Where else would he stay?" The inn was the only commercial lodging on the small island.

"I don't know," she said, walking to the check-in desk. "I'm not sure we have any available rooms."

"That's news to me." Cookie moved to look over Rain's shoulder at the reservation software. "Did we get some unexpected drop-ins?" If they had, Cookie would have to give Hunter her room, and she'd bunk with Scarlett. Or stay with Dylan. No. She couldn't do that. She hadn't spent a night at his place yet, and this wasn't how she wanted the first time to happen.

"No. But the only available room is the one I was going to repaint this week," Rain said, a petulant look on her face.

"Repaint… what?" Since when had her mother ever painted anything? They usually hired Dylan to do those tasks. Cookie scanned the software and noted the only available room was the one across from Cookie's. Ah, that was it. Rain was worried about Cookie and Hunter sharing the same floor. She shook her head and gave her mother a warning look. "It'll wait." She grabbed a key off the hook behind her and handed it to Hunter. "You can stay in the room across from mine on the third floor."

Hunter's lips turned up into a slow smile. "Thanks. I'll just go drop off my luggage then we can have some lunch and discuss the case."

The three women watched him go, none of them saying a word. Then Rain let out an exaggerated sigh. "I guess Winter and I'll go change into more *appropriate* attire." She gave Cookie a pointed look. "We wouldn't want the guests thinking we run a loose establishment here."

Cookie refrained from rolling her eyes, mostly because her stomach was growling from the aroma of Rain's pea soup, and said, "I'll go finish lunch."

By the time the bowls were out and bread was on the table Rain returned to the kitchen. She opened the fridge and grabbed butter as she said, "Poor Winter is so distraught about Blake still being in jail I thought she needed a little alone time. She's lying down in my room.

Please tell me you're close to getting this all sorted out."

Steam rose from the bowl of soup Cookie handed her mother. "I'm afraid things aren't looking so good right now." Rain's eyes widened in surprise, and she waited for Cookie to say more. "Blake's name is on the storage facility paperwork. Apparently he's the one who has been renting it all these years."

"No way!" exclaimed Winter as she walked into the kitchen. "There has to be some mistake. Not only does he not like lingerie, but Blake is also claustrophobic." Her eyes hardened as she stated, "It's clear he's being framed."

"Or perhaps he's developed those aversions since he killed Lydia," Hunter said as he strolled into the room. He walked over to Cookie and took the bowl she handed him.

Winter looked ready to claw out Hunter's eyes and before she launched herself at the man, Cookie cut in. "It *is* possible Blake was framed." Winter gave Hunter a smug look before Cookie could divert them in another direction. "Did you know Lydia?" she asked Winter.

"I knew who she was."

"Can you recall her having any close girlfriends? Someone who Lydia may have confided in?"

Winter frowned for a moment before she said, "I do recall seeing her at the Salty Dog from time to time with Pam Stevens. She's a school teacher. Third grade I think." She glanced at Rain and lowered her voice as if somehow Hunter and Cookie wouldn't hear. "Pam likes my Spring Frolic tea blend. Says it helps her unwind after a long day with children."

Rain gave her a knowing nod as she slurped up a spoonful of soup. It made Cookie think there might be more than a little chamomile in the tea Winter was talking about.

"And Julie Taylor." Winter chuckled. "She's never set foot in my shop. Probably drinks Earl Gray. She runs the historical society."

Cookie looked at Hunter. "We should try to get to them before they hear about Lydia."

"Agreed," Hunter said as he strode over to the counter and set his empty bowl down with a thud. "Ready?"

Cookie spooned in a few quick mouthfuls of her lunch as she stood up and walked over to the sink. She eyed the platter of shortbread cookies she hadn't had a chance to get to. "Sounds like a plan." She reached out and snagged a cookie. She thought about how Hunter doubted Blake's innocence and wondered if his pessimism had to do with the approaching holiday. While Cookie wasn't full of herself, she was aware that her choosing Dylan over him had to sting. She felt sympathy for her former partner, a man she loved, even if it wasn't romantic. She grabbed a couple more cookies with the hope they'd sweeten the bitterness Hunter was holding onto, and she followed him out of the inn.

10.

R AIN'S COOKIES SEEMED to do the trick, because
once Hunter and Cookie arrived at Pam's house
with the help of an Internet search for the address,
Hunter cracked a smile. When the car ignition clicked
off Cookie asked, "What's so funny?"

"Your mother has quite a sense of style."

Cookie chuckled as the vision of Rain in her purple
sequins came to mind. Then she let out an internal groan
when she remembered her mother's choice for a
microphone. "She certainly does."

Hunter climbed out of the car and gazed at the small
cape-style house before them. It was sided with natural
cedar shingles that had aged to a pale shade of grey. A
blue economy car was in the driveway, which indicated
Pam was likely home. He pushed his Ray bans up on his
nose, making Cookie note how sexy he was with his cool
exterior. The man really would be a catch for the right
woman. He deserved to have love in his life, and Cookie
was sure with a little time he'd find it. Her heart

clenched a little when she realized that when he did, he'd probably be glad Cookie hadn't chosen him instead of Dylan.

"Let's go see if we can save Winter's Valentine's Day," Hunter said.

Cookie grinned at him. "Hunter O'Neil, you're a romantic."

He mumbled as his feet crunched over ice and snow on the side of the road. "Tell anyone, Charlie, and you die."

She chuckled as she followed him to the front door of Pam's house.

Once they rang the doorbell, an older woman who was dressed in a pleated wool skirt and sweater set greeted them. A pair of glasses hung from a beaded chain on her neck. "Ms. Stevens?" Hunter asked.

"Yes. I am she."

Hunter's voice deepened to a serious tone as he flashed his badge. "I'm agent O'Neil and this is Cookie James. We'd like to ask you a few questions concerning an investigation."

"Goodness," Pam Stevens said as she put her glasses on and leaned in to read Hunter's badge. "FBI." The woman let out a small gasp as she placed her hand on her chest. "Of course." She pulled the door open and stepped to the side. "Come on in."

Cookie noted that the kind of person who was willing to talk to the FBI without asking what they'd done was either very good at lying or so innocent they squeaked. Pam struck her as the latter. The woman led Cookie and Hunter to a couch and placed herself in a chair across the coffee table from them. "Is this about one of my students?"

"No," said Cookie. "Ms. Stevens—"

"Call me Pam. Please."

Cookie continued, "Pam, we have a few questions about Lydia Rosen."

"Oh." Pam's face fell. "You found her?" She let out a sigh. "Is she in some kind of trouble?"

Cookie smiled at the woman. Pam was so sweet she didn't even assume the worst. She was curious why Pam thought Lydia might be in trouble, and so was Hunter.

"No. But what makes you ask?" Hunter said.

"Oh dear." Pam wrung her hands. "I fear I let the cat out of the bag, didn't I?" She scowled "Lydia was—" She glanced down at her feet and continued in a hushed tone, "having an affair, and I assumed when she went missing that she'd run off with her lover."

While confirmation of a lover indicated that the storage unit love nest wasn't for Blake and Lydia, it still didn't clear Blake. It pointed to a possible crime of passion instead. Declaring Blake innocent was getting more and more difficult. Cookie asked, "Do you know who Lydia's lover was?"

Pam shook her head. "No. Julie and I—" She gave them a sheepish smile. "We were curious, but Lydia was very good at keeping her secret because we had no idea."

"Julie?" asked Hunter. He knew better than to

assume anything in an investigation, even though it was likely she meant Julie Taylor.

"Julie Taylor," Pam said as she frowned. "The three of us used to be close, but it fell apart when Lydia went missing."

"Why was that?" Cookie asked.

Pam let out a huff of air. "Julie saw Lydia's disappearance as a way to get to Blake." She shook her head. "Now, I certainly don't approve of what Lydia was doing, but Julie moved in so quickly it was embarrassing. Poor Blake thought something awful had happened to his wife, and there was Julie, trying to take Lydia's place. I didn't know it at the time, but come to find out Julie and Blake dated in high school."

"I see," Hunter said thoughtfully.

"It was a waste of her time, though," Pam said. "Blake wasn't the least bit interested. She eventually gave up."

What Pam told them did cast doubt on Julie, but Cookie knew there were two sides to every story and asked, "Do you still see Julie regularly?"

Pam shook her head. "Without Lydia it was clear Julie and I didn't have too much in common." She quickly added, "Not that we're enemies or anything." She tilted her head as suspicion clouded her face. "What are all these questions about? What's going on with Lydia?"

Breaking the news of someone's death was never easy, but before Cookie could come up with a tactful way for such a kind woman to hear the worst kind of news, Hunter said, "I'm sorry to be the one to break the news, but Lydia has passed."

Pam gasped. "Dead? Oh my. What happened? Was she murdered? Is that why you're asking me so many questions?"

"I'm afraid we can't reveal the details just yet," Cookie said. "But yes, this is a homicide investigation. Can you think of anyone who might want to harm Lydia?"

Pam shook her head as tears glistened in her eyes. "No. She may not have been a faithful wife, but Lydia was a nice person. She certainly wasn't the type people would want dead."

Hunter rose to indicate the interview was over, and he held his business card out toward Pam. "If you think of anything else, please give me a call. Thank you so much for your time, Pam."

"Of course," Pam said. A tissue magically appeared from her sleeve, and she dabbed at her eyes as she stood as well.

When they got to the door Cookie said, "We're very sorry for your loss."

"You too, dear," she said as she tugged Cookie into an embrace that sucked the air out of her lungs. Cookie patted the woman's back lightly, aware that the hug was for Pam's own comfort. And she hoped she could hold on long enough before she passed out from lack of air. It was Hunter clearing his throat that finally saved her.

Cookie took a deep breath when the woman released her and she said, "Thank you, Pam."

Once they got to the car Hunter said, "Winter was right that Blake was not fooling around in the storage locker, but it still doesn't clear him of Lydia's murder."

"Agreed." Cookie gazed out the window of the Mustang. "And I think we can cross Pam off the suspect list. That woman is sweeter than Rain's cookies."

Hunter smiled. "Maybe, but I bet she knows how to rap a wayward boy's knuckles if necessary."

"What?" Cookie chuckled as she pictured Hunter in the third grade. "I bet if said boy presented her with a frog…"

"Or pulled Isabella's ponytail."

"So you're telling me you've been teasing girls all your life?"

Hunter raised his eyebrows at her and offered her a sly smile. Cookie's thoughts returned to the investigation. Discovering that Julie wanted Blake for herself was definitely interesting. She recalled a recent case they had on the island where a pastry chef poisoned a cheating lover with cheesecake. For Winter's sake, Cookie hoped Julie might be just as vindictive. "Let's go find out what Julie Taylor thinks about the news of Lydia's death." Something told Cookie this interview would go quite differently than the one they'd just had.

11.

THE TRIP TO the historical society from Pam's house brought Cookie and Hunter back by the inn. As they approached it, Hunter slowed down, and Cookie frowned when she realized why.

Up ahead was one very familiar car. A sedan with a bar of blue lights on the top was parked askew in front of the inn, and it belonged to Deputy Swan. "What is he doing here?" Cookie asked as Hunter pulled to a stop. Her stomach sank as she imagined what he might want. She'd never met a more useless human being. It was likely he wanted them to take on another investigation he was too lazy to complete or was there to share information that was totally irrelevant. Either way, the idea of the man alone with Rain and Winter didn't sit well with Cookie.

"I don't know," Hunter said. "But we'd better get in there and find out."

They stepped into the foyer to discover Rain and Winter in the living room with Deputy Swan. He was in the middle of telling a story, and the two women were giggling like school girls. "What's going on here?" Cookie asked.

Swan looked at her, and she noticed he had a drink in his hand. "Just sharing a little holiday cheer."

"You just stopped by for a visit?" Cookie asked.

"Y-yes," he slurred. "Your mother in—"

Rain interrupted. "Archie was just telling us about the time he chased a suspect into a hen house." She leaned forward as she spoke and placed her hand on Swan's knee, making her ample assets practically fall out of her shirt. The top three buttons were undone, showing off her red pushup bra.

"Mother!" Cookie exclaimed. When Rain gazed at her in confusion, Cookie hissed, "Your blouse."

"Oh," Rain giggled as she tugged it shut. She winked at Swan. "More than a few feathers get loose in this hen house, don't they?"

"This can't be happening," Cookie muttered as she walked over to the sitting area. Ice rattled in Swan's glass as she took it from his hand. "Party time is over. You should go."

"Cookie," Hunter said in a low voice as he stood behind her. "Perhaps some coffee before he gets behind the wheel."

"Right." She sighed and looked over at Winter with the hope her mother's friend might have a saner outlook on the current situation. "Can you handle this? I'd like to have a word with my mother."

"Of course." She stood. "Archie, let's move to the kitchen so I can make us some coffee and you can finish your story."

Hunter helped Winter direct Swan to the kitchen, and Cookie gazed at Rain. Her mother was definitely a loose cannon, and she'd done many a crazy thing, but trying to seduce Deputy Swan was too much. She suspected this was a ploy for Rain and Winter to get Swan to let them in to see Blake. While Swan may not be very effective, he was still a man of the law. It made Cookie wonder why she ever left her mother alone, because she and Winter were playing with fire when it came to Swan.

"Mother," she said. "I think I know what's going on here, but you and Winter really do need to be patient."

"Of course, dear," Rain said. "We do trust you. It's just that…" She let out a sigh. "Never mind. You're right, and I'm sorry."

When Rain was contrite, it never failed to chill the heat of Cookie's anger. She knew her mother was only trying to help her best friend, no matter how crazy her plans may be. Cookie walked over to her mother and pulled her into a hug. "You have a huge heart, Mom, and I know you meant well. But some things you shouldn't try to fix."

"I know. I'm sorry."

Hunter stepped back into the room. "Everything under control, Charlie?"

Cookie nodded. "We'll be back soon, Mom. Call me

if you have any problems."

When they got back outside, Hunter suggested they walk to town since they were so close. Cookie agreed and welcomed the chill of the frosty air on her cheeks. The island appeared as if someone had laid out a white fluffy blanket, and the sun sparkled on its surface like tiny threads of gold weaved in the fabric. She'd never thought of herself as a nature girl, but her time on the island had given her an appreciation for the outdoors.

Cookie had traded her love for the excitement and bustle of the city for small town life where the air was clear and the pace was slower. She knew Dylan had too, and she thought about how he was cooped up inside viewing boring security tapes from Sunfish storage facility. Her skin prickled with irritation, knowing it was because Hunter didn't want to be around him.

She spied a stationery shop ahead, and it hit her that Valentine's Day was coming and she hadn't even gotten Dylan a card. While Cookie knew she should be sensitive to Hunter's feelings, she was afraid with the way the investigation was going she might not get another chance, so she said, "I need to take a quick detour."

When they pushed open the door to the shop, a small bell rang to announce their arrival. Cookie noticed an older man behind the counter as she made a beeline for the racks of cards.

Hunter chuckled when she began to read the offerings in the Valentine's Day section. "I'm not sure why you're bothering, Charlie," he said as he reached over her shoulder for one. He opened up his card, and let out a low noise of disgust. "Dylan isn't the kind of guy to get you a card."

"How do you know?" Still irritated that she wasn't with Dylan, Cookie nudged Hunter and quipped, "If you hadn't given him hours of the Sunfish's security tapes to watch maybe he could."

Ignoring her question, Hunter grabbed another card which immediately started to play a song, and he snapped it shut as if it were about to bite him.

"Did you say something about the Sunfish security tapes?" squeaked out a voice, and Cookie looked over at the sales clerk who had walked over to them.

His hair was thinning on the top, and he was dressed in a button down shirt and sweater vest. Cookie recalled meeting him at a chamber of commerce meeting a few months ago and knew he was the owner of the shop. "Andy, right?" she asked.

He nodded. "You're Cookie James from the inn. And you—" Andy paused to swallow hard as he gazed at Hunter, and the color drained from his face. "You're that FBI agent. Did someone die?"

Hunter gave him a cold stare. "At the moment, I'm just a man buying a Valentine's Day card."

A sheen of moisture covered Andy's face. "Right. I suppose you can't talk about that sort of thing."

"No," Cookie said as she smiled sweetly at him. She handed him her card. "I'll take this please."

Hunter shoved the musical card toward Andy as well.

"She wants this one too."

Cookie would have made a crack at Hunter, but she noticed Andy sway a little as he made his way behind the register. "Are you all right?" she asked.

Andy turned to face her. "I—I don't know. I think I might be coming down with the flu."

While Cookie was sympathetic to the man's plight, she was anxious to get out of there quickly. She and Dylan had plans for Valentine's Day that she had no intention of missing, and getting the flu wasn't on her agenda. "I hope you feel better," she offered as Andy rang her up, and Hunter must have had the same aversion to getting sick as she did, because he was already holding the door open when Cookie took her bag.

They both inhaled deeply once they were outside. The icy air in her lungs invigorated Cookie enough that she was able to tease Hunter. "Who did I just buy a card for, Hunter?"

"Wouldn't you like to know?" He quipped back so quickly it made Cookie chuckle.

"What are we," she asked, "twelve?"

He shrugged but didn't offer any more information, and since they were at their destination, Cookie let it drop.

12.

THE HISTORICAL SOCIETY was aptly located in one of the island's oldest buildings and was a testament to Julie Taylor's attention to detail, because it was impeccably maintained. Hunter's and Cookie's feet scraped across the bone-dry granite steps where a red wreath of winter berries adorned the door. The centuries-old hinges barely let out a groan as they entered.

The lobby was set up with photographs on both pedestals and the walls as a museum of the town's history, but it was the woman at the back of the room that captured Cookie's attention. She was dressed in deep-red skirt and jacket with a perfectly-coiffed hairdo reminiscent of Jackie Kennedy. Cookie suspected even a strong wind couldn't blow a hair out of place. She recalled seeing the woman at chamber of commerce meetings like she had Andy, and she knew she was gazing at Julie Taylor.

"Good afternoon, folks," the woman said as she approached them. "Are you here to learn more about

Secret Seal Island?" She gave Hunter a large smile. "I may have a rogue pirate story or two to share."

Hunter took the bait, and he wasn't above using his charm to get answers. "I'm sure I'd enjoy hearing them, Miss…"

"*Miss* Julie Taylor," she said as she held out her hand.

Hunter took it in both of his hands. "Miss Taylor, I'm Hunter O'Neil from the FBI and this is Cookie James. We'd like to ask you some questions."

Julie flinched, and Cookie was impressed with the restraint Julie showed when she didn't yank her fingers out of his grasp. Hunter let her go, and she frowned as if she was confused. "FBI. In our town?" She glanced at Cookie and the skin around her eyes crinkled as she narrowed them. "You and your mother moved here about a year ago to take over ownership of the inn, didn't you?"

Cookie had a good idea where Julie was going and held back a laugh. "That's right."

"It seems you brought some excitement along with you," Julie said. "Do you know that before you arrived there hadn't been a murder on this island since old Jed Keezer shot his best friend in a hunting accident about fifty years ago?"

"You don't say," Hunter said. "I bet you know a lot about what happens in this town."

Julie turned her attention to him. "I do."

Hunter gave her his killer smile. "I've clearly come to the right place. Is there somewhere we can sit and talk?"

Julie dropped her gaze as a slight flush rose to her cheeks. "Right this way." She turned and sauntered over to a hallway, her hips positively sashaying in a skirt Cookie noted was tight around the woman's bottom.

She led them to small conference room and took a place at the head of the table. Cookie and Hunter sat on either side. Cookie was tempted to launch into the line of questioning, but she knew that they'd get more if Hunter did the talking, so she leaned back to let him take the lead.

"We're here to ask you a few questions about Lydia Rosen," Hunter said.

Julie blinked as if she was in shock, or trying to hide she wasn't.

Cookie narrowed her line of vision to watch the woman closely.

"Lydia Rosen," Julie said. "I haven't spoken to her in years, but I'm happy to tell you anything I know."

"You two were quite close at one point," Hunter said. "Yes?"

"We were." Julie folded her hands on top of the table.

So that's how this is going to go, Cookie thought as a small smile formed on her face. While Julie may have thought she had the upper hand, doling out whatever information she felt like sharing, Cookie knew better. Hunter would get her talking one way or the other, and she settled in to watch the show.

"Tell me about your friendship," Hunter said.

Julie shrugged. "We met for lunch, went to the movies and out to dinner occasionally. You know." She gave Hunter a flirty smile. "The kinds of things *women* do."

"Yes. I do know," Hunter said with a suggestive tone as he flirted right back. "So she confided in you too."

"Yes. To a point."

Cookie found it interesting that Julie wasn't asking questions of her own, and she decided to get the ball of this conversation rolling. "We talked to Pam Stevens earlier, and she told us you two speculated about why Lydia disappeared. Care to elaborate?"

Julie's mouth tightened. "I'm sure Pam told you everything there is to know."

Cookie lobbed the ball perfectly because Hunter said, "Really. You don't strike me as the kind of woman who lets anyone talk for her." Julie's nostrils flared making her anger apparent, and Hunter hit it home. "Especially a woman like Pam Stevens."

"Pam is a busybody," Julie snapped. "Lydia just up and skipped town with some man and left her heartbroken husband behind." Julie's eyes flashed with her anger. "All I was trying to do was offer Blake some comfort, but you'd think I was the reason Lydia left by the way Pam acted."

Julie's outburst told Cookie she didn't appear to know Lydia was dead. That meant unless Julie was an excellent liar, she wasn't the killer. Unfortunately, Cookie couldn't write her off with absolute certainty. It was only weeks ago they'd both been fooled by another case.

After they gave Julie a moment to calm down, Cookie spoke in a sympathetic tone. "I'm sure it was painful to lose two friends in such a short time."

Julie sighed as she looked at Cookie. "It was. The three of us had been so close." She shook her head. "I never realized how jealous Pam was of me."

Cookie nodded, and Hunter glanced at her as he said, "Jealousy *can* break up friendships. It's tough to keep it from happening."

Cookie offered him a smile to let him know she understood he was apologizing for his actions earlier in his own way.

"You haven't told me why you're asking all these questions," Julie said. "What's going on?"

"I'm afraid we have some bad news for you." Hunter paused to let her prepare for the worst. "We're investigating Lydia Rosen's murder."

The woman's face paled. "Oh my gosh. Oh. Poor Blake. This is terrible news." Her expression was earnest as she stared in Hunter's eyes. "How did he take it? I really should go see him. I'm sure he could use a friend right now."

Cookie almost burst out in laughter. She had to give Julie credit, though. The woman certainly was tenacious. But once she got past her initial amusement, Cookie thought that Julie's obsession with Blake made her look more and more like a potential suspect. Was it possible she'd killed Lydia with the intent of moving in on Blake? The idea seemed unreasonable, but after her years working for the FBI, Cookie had seen people do crazier things when it came to jealousy and matters of the heart.

Julie sat up a little straighter and tugged on her suit jacket, clearly ready for the interview to be over. "Now. If we're done here I have some work I must get to."

"One more question," Hunter said. "Can you think of anyone who might want to harm Lydia?"

Julie's brow knitted as she took a moment to think, and then she shook her head. "No. I can't think of anyone who didn't like Lydia. I'm sorry."

"Thank you for being so cooperative." Hunter reached into his suit jacket and produced a business card. "If you think of anything that could be helpful, give me a call."

Julie licked her lips and smiled up at him. "I believe you just gave me your number."

Hunter chuckled as he led the way out of the room, and Cookie held back the urge to whisper to Julie to go ahead and call him. Her former partner had always had a way with women, and clearly being jilted by Cookie hadn't affected his charm and confidence one bit.

When they got outside, Cookie finally let herself laugh.

"What's so funny, Charlie?"

"I'm just trying to sort out which woman you're hoping will call, Pam or Julie?"

Hunter scoffed. "Please. You know I prefer a bigger

challenge. A slow burn if you will." He swept his gaze over her, taking his time, making it all too clear he was talking about her. "Not to mention hotter, curvier, and an expert with a deadly weapon."

Despite the chill in the air, her entire body heated. She glanced away, annoyed at her reaction. Annoyed at him for crossing the line. And most of all, annoyed at herself for opening the door on the conversation when questioning which woman he was interested in. Cookie cleared her throat and glanced away.

Hunter laughed. "Damn, you're cute when you're embarrassed."

Cookie turned and glared at him. "You know this isn't appropriate. I'm with—"

He held up his hand, shaking his head. "No need to say it. I know all too well who you're dating." Frowning, he peered at her. "You don't need to get so worked up, Charlie. This is just me and you as we've always been—inappropriate banter that means nothing and goes nowhere. Unless you've decided that's off limits now, too." He paused for a moment. "Is it? If so, tell me now."

Cookie was quiet as she processed what he'd said. He was right. The entire time they'd been partners, they'd ribbed each other and neither had been shy on the innuendo. In the beginning, it hadn't meant anything. But later it had. And it definitely did when they'd been deciding if they wanted to start something. Did it matter if the banter continued? Certainly Dylan wouldn't appreciate it if he thought Hunter was hitting on her.

Finally, she sighed. "I don't know, Hunter. Everything's changed, and maybe it's just too soon for us to go there right now."

He pressed his lips together and nodded.

She opened her mouth to say something more, anything to lighten the mood and get them off the current subject. But her phone buzzed with a text, and she pulled it out of her pocket. "It's Dylan. He's done going through the security tapes."

"Good. Have him meet us back at the inn," Hunter said and started walking.

Cookie quickly tapped out a message to Dylan, and scowling at Hunter's back, she stretched her long legs and followed.

13.

THE LIGHTS GLOWED from the pretty Victorian inn as Cookie and Hunter walked up the hill. Dylan's truck was parked in the driveway, and the delicious scent of savory beef filled Cookie's senses, making her stomach growl.

With a completely full inn, no doubt Rain was busy cooking up a storm for whoever was milling around. Normally Cookie welcomed having people around. It meant the inn was bringing in an income, something they hadn't actually excelled at much during the first year. But tonight she just wanted to curl up by the fireplace with her best friend Scarlett and forget the earlier exchange with Hunter. Too bad that wasn't in the cards.

As Cookie was reaching for the knob, the door swung open and Dylan stood there with a lazy smile on his face.

"Hello, gorgeous," he said, pulling her inside.

Hunter let out a barely audible grunt of irritation but

said nothing.

Cookie ignored him and smiled up at Dylan. He had a glint in his steel blue eyes. *What is he up to*, Cookie wondered? "Hey, yourself."

His hand tightened around hers as he nodded civilly to Hunter.

Hunter shrugged out of his outerwear, barely acknowledging Dylan and gave Scarlett, who was sitting by the fire, a slow lazy grin. "Scar, what's going on?"

The tall fair-haired beauty was wearing skinny jeans, a formfitting sweater, and stylish faux-fur boots. Even dressed down she looked like she'd just stepped out of a magazine. She held up a stack of photos. "Working on my portfolio."

Hunter raised an eyebrow. "Does this mean you've given up on law for good?"

Scarlett was a high-powered lawyer with her own firm in New York City. Or she had been until she'd skipped out a few months earlier and decided to stay with Cookie on Secret Seal Island. It was meant to be short term, but she'd taken up photography and hadn't found a way to leave yet. "I think so," Scarlett said quietly. "I'm certainly not ready to go back, and I need something to keep my mind sharp."

Dylan helped Cookie out of her coat, and the pair of them watched as Hunter made his way to the couch and sat next to Scarlett. He leaned in and studied her shots. "I don't know much about photography beyond crime-scene shots, but these look really good."

A pleased smile claimed Scarlett's lips and her eyes lit up as she said, "Thank you. Which do you think is the most eye-catching? I'm trying to figure out which one to use on my business card."

"This one." He tapped a photo lying on the coffee table. Cookie squinted, trying to make out the image. It was picture of Scarlett herself, naked from the waist up, showing only her back and she was walking right out into the cold Maine waters. It was an overcast day and clearly cold, judging by the gooseflesh covering her skin and the white caps on the water, but she was jumping, her hands raised in the air and her head tilted back, exuding joy. She'd said it was a representation of embracing life.

"Why?" Scarlett asked.

Hunter reached out and tucked a lock of hair behind her ear. "Because you're baring yourself for the world to see."

"I *am* topless," she said with a smirk.

He chuckled. "I noticed." Almost as if he was unable to help himself, he swept his gaze over her the way Cookie had seen him do a thousand times before when he was interested in someone. Then as if he'd caught himself, he blinked and his expression cleared. "It's what's interesting about it. You're half dressed, but that's not what we see. Not really."

Scarlett's face flushed pink, and she said, "Thank you."

Dylan shot Cookie a curious glance as the pair

moved on to animatedly debate the best shots of the island. "What's going on there?" Dylan whispered.

Cookie shrugged. "No idea." It was strange watching Hunter take such an interest in Scarlett. It wasn't as if he'd ignored her before, but the way his knee was pressed against hers, combined with the undeniable interest in his gaze, made Cookie realize Hunter wasn't just being nice. Whether he knew it or not, he was flirting with Scarlett, something he'd never done before. At least not with Cookie around.

And to Cookie's surprise, she realized she didn't mind. She'd expected to feel a pang of jealousy when Hunter moved on, considering how strong her feelings for him had been only months ago. The fact was Hunter and Cookie had been so close as partners they could finish each other's sentences and predict what the other would do in most situations. It would only be natural for Cookie to at least feel slighted when another woman finally captured his undivided attention.

But she felt neither of those things. Cookie discovered she felt relief. Especially after the awkward banter they'd experienced earlier in the day. So much so that she welcomed his interest in someone other than her... for both their sakes.

"Come on." Cookie took Dylan's hand in hers and tugged him toward the kitchen. "Let's see if Rain needs any help."

As Cookie and Dylan passed through the dining room, Cookie smiled at the half-dozen guests sitting at the table enjoying Rain's famous crab stuffed mushrooms. There were murmurs of appreciation when Cookie asked how everyone was doing. She grinned and promised to relay their compliments to the chef.

"When did Rain start making dinner for everyone?" Dylan asked as they crossed into the kitchen.

"I've always invited them," Rain answered from her spot at the island. "It's just that now we actually have people to serve." She grinned. "They love me."

"They certainly do," Cookie agreed. "They're singing your praises over the mushrooms."

Rain let out a mischievous snicker and immediately, Cookie became suspicious.

"Mother, please tell me you didn't feed them special mushrooms," Cookie demanded. Rain got into all kinds of trouble with Winter, but Cookie never dreamed her mother would unknowingly drug anyone.

"Of course not. Who do you think I am?" Rain asked, her hands balling into fists as she set them on her hips.

"I think that sometimes your new identity, Rain Forest, has had more of an effect on you than is advisable."

"Pshaw." Rain waved a hand and went back to slicing a load of artisan bread. "Please. I'm as responsible as the next guy."

"Then what was with the sly smile, then?" Cookie demanded.

Dylan reached over and grabbed one of the

mushrooms in question. After sniffing it, he shrugged. "Smells normal to me."

Rain's head popped up and she stared at him, a challenge written all over her face. "Go ahead, try it. Then let Cookie know if I altered it."

Dylan glanced between the two of them, hesitating. Cookie watched him with one eyebrow raised. Surely her mother wouldn't drug Dylan. Right?

Rain put her knife down, pressed her hands to the counter and waited. "No dinner until you eat the mushroom."

That was good enough for Dylan. He popped the appetizer in his mouth and chewed. A look of pure rapture transformed his features and he actually let out a tiny moan of pleasure.

Cookie's face flushed as she wished with everything she had that she'd been the bite of food in his mouth. Anything that could elicit that response was well worth the effort.

Rain pressed a hand to her heart and she let out a dreamy sigh. "Now that's exactly what I was going for when I made those. Cookie, do you see that look on his face?"

"Yeah," Cookie said quietly, unable to tear her gaze away.

"That's why I was smiling. Foodgasm at its finest." Rain's eyes glittered with satisfaction, and Cookie had to hand it to her. She'd certainly outdone herself.

If Hunter wasn't still in the other room waiting to

find out what was on the security tapes from the storage unit, Cookie would've been sorely tempted to take Dylan and the rest of the mushrooms right up to her bedroom. Who needed dinner when the appetizers appeared to be the main show?

"I think our guests are going to have a *really* nice night, don't you?" Rain asked Dylan. "The last time I fed that dish to Hale, he couldn't wait to rip my clothes off and—"

"That's enough," Cookie said. "Congratulations on your aphrodisiac mushrooms, Mom. I'm sure they're a huge hit."

Dylan nodded, grinning at her like an overzealous teenager.

She ignored him and the tingle in her belly that had her wanting to pull him upstairs. And she hadn't even had a bite of the titillating appetizer. Good gracious, she needed to get a hold of herself. "I'm just going to grab a tray for us, Scarlett, and Hunter." Dylan raised his eyebrows at her and she quickly added, "But no more mushrooms."

"That's a shame," Dylan muttered.

Rain laughed and picked up the bread basket. "Trays are where they usually are. Help yourself while I take the bread to the paying guests."

Cookie and Dylan went to work spooning the hearty stew into hand-thrown pottery soup bowls. With four servings ready to go, Cookie added a basket of bread, butter, and utensils. Four bottles of beer clinked as

Dylan gathered them, and they made their way back to the living room where Scarlett and Hunter had a pile of Scarlett's photo's set aside. They were debating the merits of the latest Star Wars movie.

Cookie cleared her throat. "Dinner."

"Thank heavens," Scarlett said, and she moved her pictures and portfolio. "I'm starving."

After placing the tray in the middle of the coffee table, Cookie grabbed a bowl and sat in a chair at the end of the table. Dylan passed out the beers and sat opposite her, leaving Hunter and Scarlett on the couch. Cookie noted her best friend and former partner weren't exactly leaving each other much in the way of personal space.

Cookie cleared her throat. "So, Dylan, did you find anything useful on the security tapes?"

Dylan tore his eyes away from Scarlett and Hunter. Apparently he'd also noticed the change in the way they interacted. But he kept his thoughts to himself and answered Cookie's question. "No. Nothing useful. The only time Lydia's unit was opened was when Rain and Winter showed up." He took a sip of his beer.

"You went through all that footage already?" Hunter asked, disbelief in his tone.

"Of course not," Dylan said, giving Hunter a what-the-hell look. "The cameras are only activated when the equipment senses movement."

"That could've been manipulated," Cookie said, thinking out loud.

Hunter shrugged. "Could've, but it's unlikely. It doesn't seem like many people around here are that tech savvy."

He might've had a point, but it had been just a month ago when they'd had to deal with a case that involved embezzlement. Tampering with security cameras couldn't be more difficult than that, could it? "Either way, we don't have any evidence of tampering, so it's a moot point," Cookie said.

Dylan shook his head. "They weren't tampered with. I checked."

Cookie eyed her boyfriend, impressed with his knowledge. He'd been in the Navy in a past life and had talents even she wasn't aware of. "What was it you did while you were a SEAL again?"

He just chuckled.

Hunter gave Dylan a nod of respect. Regardless of the former rivalry between them, Cookie knew Hunter respected the skills Dylan brought to the table. At least they had that going for them.

"What about the neighboring units? Did you get in touch with the renters?" Cookie asked.

Dylan said, "I did, and the owners of twelve and fourteen never had a reason to give unit thirteen a second glance."

"That exhausts our leads at the Sunfish then," said Hunter.

"While you were going through mind-numbing security tapes," Cookie said to Dylan, "we visited Lydia's two friends, Pam and Julie."

"Pam is clean," Hunter offered, and took a swig of his beer. "I'd bet cash money she didn't have anything to do with Lydia's death."

Cookie nodded her agreement. "Same. Pam is sweet as pie. I just don't see it. Julie, on the other hand—"

"The jealousy runs deep with that one," Hunter said.

"Is it strong enough to lead to murder?" Dylan asked, leaning forward.

Cookie grabbed a piece of her rosemary herb bread and spread a thick slab of butter over the surface. "She did go after Blake right after Lydia disappeared. She also seemed to really despise Lydia for having an affair. It's as good a motive as any."

"So where does that leave us?" Dylan asked.

"Nowhere really," Cookie said. "It's just a theory. We need to do some more investigative work."

Hunter nodded. "I put in the paperwork for a warrant to search Blake's home. It's supposed to be ready tomorrow. Winter said Lydia had a journal, and we need to see what's in it."

Cookie nodded. "So that's where we'll start tomorrow." With a solid plan in place, Cookie finally took a large bite of the bread she was still holding and had to hold back a moan of pleasure. It was fresh and still slightly warm.

"Got enough butter there, Charlie?" Hunter asked with a teasing twinkle in his eye.

"No." Cookie gave him a defiant look and added

more of the creamy goodness to the bread.

"I always did like a woman with a little meat on her bones," Dylan said with a wink.

Cookie blushed, but it didn't stop her from taking a big bite. "This is delicious," she mumbled.

Scarlett laughed and touched a red nail-polished finger to the corner of her mouth, indicating Cookie had dabbed herself with butter.

"Goodness, Cookie!" Rain called as she entered the room and caught her daughter wiping her mouth with the back of her hand. "You'd think I raised you with no manners at all."

"Charlie has manners... not when she's eating, though." Hunter gave Cookie a knowing glance. "I've never seen a woman pack it away like she does."

"With gusto?" Dylan chimed in.

"Hey!" Cookie said, not sure if she should be offended or amused that they were ganging up on her. "I'm not that bad."

"Sure." Hunter laughed. "Remember that time we were eating kielbasa in that pub in Philly? You snorted a laugh and a piece of it flew out of your nose. It was the grossest and most hilarious thing I've ever seen."

The room cackled with laughter.

Cookie gave them all a flat stare as a faint memory of the spicy sausage burning her nasal passages came back to her. As soon as they quieted down she said, "And I seem to recall that little maneuver of mine threw our perp off his game, and we ended up catching him red-handed in a felony drug transaction."

"Damn," Scarlett said, her laughter gone now as her expression switched over to awe. "Cookie, you're a badass."

"Yes, she is," both Dylan and Hunter responded at the same time, their tone sobering as well. The room went quiet, and all they heard was the light din from the guests still congregated in the dining room.

After the awkward silence stretched out a beat or two, Rain, who could always be counted on to lighten the mood, said, "Well, of course she is. She takes after me. Did I ever tell you about the time I caught old man Peterman stuffing zucchinis in his Dockers at the farmer's market?" She mimed sliding the phallic vegetables into her pants and swayed her hips. "He said he was just trying to keep his hands free because he had more shopping to do, but we all knew what was going on. There was a social at the historical society later that day and he was trying to impress the ladies."

Dylan and Scarlett busted up with laughter while Hunter acted as if the story pained him. Cookie leaned back in her chair, tuning out the rest of the story. She'd heard it before. Mr. Peterman had offered to let someone give him a strip search, but the organizers had just ordered him to pay the zucchini vendor and then he was banned from the premises.

She watched Hunter pretending disinterest, but as he watched Scarlett leaning forward, egging Rain on, he started to smile and let his guard down. Hunter had always acted as if Rain gave him heartburn. He had a hard time letting anyone see beyond his cool FBI exterior, but Cookie'd always suspected Hunter was secretly amused by her mother. And why wouldn't he be? While often ridiculous, she was extremely entertaining. It was one of the things Cookie loved most about Rain. That and her huge heart.

Cookie's gaze met Dylan's and she was surprised to see he was watching her instead of devoting his attention to Rain. His lips curved into a smile then he raised his eyebrows in question as he jerked his head toward the front door and mouthed, *Porch?*

Nodding, Cookie stood and collected the dinner dishes back onto the tray. Dylan pitched in and while Rain was still rattling on about old man Peterman, they bypassed the inn guests still enjoying dessert and coffee and retreated to the already cleaned kitchen.

"Rain appears to be Wonder Woman," Dylan said, jumping in to rinse the bowls.

Warmth spread through Cookie. Her mother really was something else, and it only made her love Dylan more that he saw it as well. "She is. Can you believe she did all this by herself? Dinner, dessert, coffee, and she's been keeping an eye on Winter. She's definitely where I get my badass gene."

Dylan grinned, and the bowls clattered as he loaded the dishwasher.

When he was done, Cookie closed the machine, worked her way between him and the sink, and wrapped her arms around him. "You're pretty great, too, you know."

His darkening eyes were his only response as his gaze dropped to her lips.

She ran her hands over his shoulders, enjoying their quiet moment together. "This is better than freezing our butts off outside."

"But if we were outside, I'd have an excuse to warm yours up," he said, his voice suddenly husky.

"Hmm, now that we're dating, I really don't think you need an excuse."

"That's good to know." He dipped his head and brushed his warm lips over hers.

Goosebumps skittered over her skin, and she leaned into him, welcoming his kiss. She felt a tingle as his hands slid down her back, and they were just about to reach the promised land when Cookie heard footsteps followed immediately by a loud, "Oops! Sorry."

Dylan released Cookie and she peered around his impressive frame to find her mother holding a tray of dishes that were teetering precariously as she was awkwardly trying to back out of the kitchen. "Mom? What are you doing?"

"Trying to give you privacy. My bad. I didn't know you two were getting busy in here, otherwise I would've left the dessert dishes for later."

"We were not—never mind." Cookie quickly crossed the room and grabbed the tray from her mother. "We've got this. You've already worked hard enough today."

"No, no," Rain said, following her daughter to the sink. "I just need to finish these up and then I'm done." She cast Dylan a quick glance and then let her gaze settle on Cookie. "You two should get back to feeling each other up."

Dylan choked out a laugh.

Cookie rolled her eyes. "Maybe later." She gently nudged her mother out of the way. "I've got this. Go put your feet up."

When Dylan took his place next to Cookie and flipped on the water to rinse dishes, Rain fluffed her curly red hair and said, "Well, if you insist." She glanced at the clock on the wall. "I think I'll go make a phone call and see if I can't find me a hot date."

"Good luck," Cookie called as Rain disappeared again.

Dylan started to laugh.

"What?" she asked as she grabbed a water-slicked plate from him to put in the dishwasher.

Dylan pointed to the clock. "It's almost eight o'clock. Your mother is officially calling Hale for a booty call."

"Oh, jeez." Cookie grimaced as she rearranged dishes to fit more into the washer. "Mood killer."

"You started it when you volunteered us for hard labor." He winked, and in a move that made her melt inside, he started wiping down the counters.

Cookie turned and crossed her arms over her chest watching him. When he was done, she said, "Sexy, handy, and domesticated. You just might be the perfect man."

He tossed the rag onto the counter and embraced her once more. "Perfect for you."

"You got that right." This time Cookie leaned in and kissed him. She didn't know how long the kiss lasted, but it was long enough to leave her breathless when Dylan finally pulled away, regret in his steel-blue gaze. "What is it?"

"I think I better go before this gets out of hand."

Cookie's eyebrows shot up as she considered dragging him to her bedroom. "Why?"

"Hunter's staying in the room across from yours, right?"

"Um, yeah." Cookie pressed her lips together and nodded. "Good point." Awkward wouldn't begin to cover it if Dylan and Hunter ran into each other in the hall on the way to the bathroom. "I'll walk you out."

As they passed through the dining room, Cookie noticed the dinner guests had retreated to their rooms and the table had been set for breakfast. Cookie really had to hand it to Rain, and she felt a twinge of guilt. Her mother worked hard to keep the inn running without much help from Cookie, since she was usually off investigating the murder of the month.

Once Dylan and Cookie reached the front door, they paused to say their goodbyes, and Cookie couldn't help noticing both Scarlett and Hunter were climbing the stairs. He was right behind her, and the two were talking and laughing softly. Were they headed to bed… together? Cookie shook her head. Did it matter? She couldn't deny that even though she'd had no problem with them flirting, she couldn't imagine Scarlett getting together with Hunter so soon after knowing he'd had feelings for her. She wasn't sure it was jealousy she was feeling, but Cookie was definitely uneasy about the situation.

She shook her head. No, she was letting her imagination run away with her.

"What is it, Cookie?" Dylan asked, eyeing her.

"Nothing. Just marveling at how things turn out." She pressed up on her toes and gave Dylan one last kiss. "See you tomorrow?"

He gave her a strange look then just said, "You can count on it."

After he left, Cookie locked the front door and retreated up the two flights of stairs to her bedroom. And when she got there, she was relieved to see Hunter's door was open, the light was on, and he was definitely alone.

She'd let her over-active imagination get the best of her. "Night, Hunter," she said.

He glanced up from his phone, nodded and said, "Night, Charlie."

14.

COOKIE WAS BARELY awake when she heard, and *felt,* her insides rumble with hunger when she put her hand on her stomach. It was because of the delicious aroma of bacon wafting up from the ground floor. If there was one thing that could get Cookie up before noon, it was bacon. She rolled out of bed, wrapped herself in her robe, and wasn't at all surprised to find Hunter was already up and gone. Likely, he'd taken off for his usual morning run.

That worked perfectly for her as she jumped in the shower and went through her morning routine. Forty minutes later, her feet tapped lightly as she descended the stairs and headed straight for the kitchen. Rain was nowhere to be seen, but there was coffee. And while there was a pan with enough bacon grease to choke a horse there was in fact, no bacon.

She was too late.

Pouting, she grabbed a leftover slice of bread from the night before and her mug of coffee before heading for the office. As long as she was waiting for Hunter, she might as well get some paperwork done to help Rain with at least some of the inn's operations.

Surprised there weren't any guests milling about, Cookie started to wonder where everyone had gone. But more specifically, she wondered where Rain was. She took a bite of her bread as she pushed on the office door with her hip.

It creaked open, and Cookie froze.

Rain, dressed in a red-sequined halter top and her leather pants that showed her butt crack, was sitting on the edge of the desk, feeding a piece of bacon to—holy crap, was that Swan? A horrifying thought hit her. Had Swan been her mother's booty call the night before?

Cookie sucked in a breath and immediately choked on the bread she'd been chewing. She couldn't breathe as her cough became uncontrollable and her eyes watered.

"Cookie!" her mother cried and jumped down from the desk.

The next thing Cookie knew, Rain's thin arms were wrapped around her middle and her mother shoved a fist against her upper stomach as she squeezed with force yelling, "Spit it out, Cookie! Spit it out!"

The clogged piece of bread immediately shot across the room and splattered on the glass window. Cookie stood there, stunned. She gulped in a mouthful of air while watching the pasty ball of food slide down the window in slow motion.

"That's disgusting," Swan said and chomped down

on a piece of bacon.

"You don't say?" Cookie rasped out.

"Oh, my god. Honey, are you okay?" Rain asked, running her hands over Cookie's arms and peering at her as if checking for hidden wounds.

Not one comfortable being fussed over, Cookie said, "It was just a piece of bread, Mom. Not shrapnel. My arms are fine." She stepped away from her mother's worrying hands.

"I just… you were choking!" Rain let out a whimper, then flung herself at Cookie, holding her tight. "Thank goodness you're all right."

"Thanks to you," Cookie said, her voice warm and grateful now that her shock had worn off. "You really know what you're doing with that Heimlich maneuver."

Rain lifted her head and beamed up at Cookie. "I told you I was paying attention in class."

Cookie chuckled, remembering scolding her mother for playing on Facebook and Twitter through the entire first-aid certification. "So you were. And good thing for me."

"You should get her one of these, *Rain Forest*," Swan said, dragging out her mother's name as he held up a mug. "This will fix her up. Whiskey fixes everything."

Cookie narrowed her eyes at the sheriff, remembering it was his presence that had nearly caused her untimely demise. "Excuse us," Cookie said and dragged Rain out of the office.

"What is it, dear?" Rain asked. Then her eyes

widened and she covered her mouth with her hand. "It's the bacon, isn't it? I forgot to leave you some."

"It's not the bacon, Mother. Though, that would've been nice."

Rain made a move to open the office door as she said, "There's some extra in here."

But Cookie stopped her. "No. I'm fine. That's not what I want to talk about." She paused, because she suddenly felt like the mother of a wayward teen who'd been busted for missing curfew. She took a deep breath and asked, "Has Swan been here all night?"

"What?" Rain looked genuinely shocked, much to Cookie's relief. "No," her mother said. "Of course not. He just came by this morning for a little Irish coffee between friends."

She gave Cookie a mischievous smile and lowered her voice. "We're building up a rapport. You know, the kind that'll loosen him up and make him see reason about letting Blake out on bail." She bit her lower lip and thrust her ample bosom out a bit. "I'm using my *womanly* charms to help Winter."

"Mother," Cookie said, rolling her eyes to the sky while praying for patience. "You can't do that. Getting him drunk and trying to persuade him to do anything is a terrible idea. You're interfering in an investigation." She gave her mother an intense, go-to-your-room type stare. "We've already had this discussion, and I thought I'd made myself perfectly clear. Now go back in there and ask him to leave. Hunter and I are doing everything we can."

Rain pouted. "But I think I was making progress."

Cookie ground her teeth. "How many ways do I have to tell you no?" Cookie wished she had the ability to ground Rain, or take her phone or her Internet privileges. Although she knew that none of those things would ever stop Rain anyway. She tried a different tactic and spoke in a softer tone. "Please get him out of here before he drinks too much and passes out. What would our guests think of the local law if they saw that?"

Rain seemed to go for that logic and nodded her head. "I think that ship may have sailed. He's already had three mugs full, and when I say Irish coffee, what I really mean is just an Irish whiskey. Goodness that man sure can put the drink away, can't he?"

Oh, hell, Cookie thought as her original anger returned. She rubbed at her temple and didn't bother to hide her feelings. "Just get him out of here, okay?"

"Fine." Rain let out a small huff of her own irritation. "I was only trying to help." She gave Cookie her mother-knows-best look. "I see you're still breathing."

Cookie sighed. "I know, Mother." Rain did have a point. It was hard to stay mad at her mother considering she was still alive because of Rain's quick thinking. Cookie took a calming breath and said, "Maybe you can help me by figuring out where Hunter might be."

Rain shrugged. "That's easy." She glanced past Cookie. "Behind you."

Cookie whirled, finding Hunter freshly showered and dressed in his signature FBI-agent suit.

He held out his hand. "Can I interest you in some breakfast?"

15.

COOKIE BLINKED AT the handsome vision of her former partner standing before her. There really was something hot about a man in a suit. Especially when Cookie knew what most of him looked like under it. She inhaled more deeply. Was that cologne she smelled? Hunter had really been turning on the charm for Scarlett the night before. Did he have plans with her friend later? The thought made her smile as she put her hand in his outstretched one and accepted his offer for breakfast. "I'd love to."

"Um-hmm," Rain grumbled from beside Cookie. Apparently her mother hadn't noticed the way Hunter had been making eyes at Scarlett and still thought he might be a threat to her relationship with Dylan.

Cookie glanced at her mother. "Well. *Somebody* did eat all the bacon." She squinted at Rain. "And don't you have something you need to do?"

"Fine." Rain huffed and went back into the office, where Swan was no doubt enjoying too much alcohol.

Hopefully she'd get Swan out of the inn and herself out of the precarious arms of the local law before she got into trouble that couldn't be fixed.

Cookie let Hunter pull her along toward the door before they released their grasp. When they stepped outside Cookie noticed it was another beautiful day on the island, with a blue sky set against the winter wonderland of white. Although, the change in temperature had made a coating of frost form on the windshield of Hunter's car. It would take longer to defrost it than it would to walk to the Salty Dog, so they set out on foot.

"What sort of trouble is your mother up to today? Or do I not want to know?" Hunter asked.

Cookie sighed. "Her usual. She's convinced she can get Swan to do as she pleases, but I think she finally understands the dangers of that."

"Good. He may be a bumbling idiot, but he does have the law on his side. I'd hate for something to happen to Rain."

"Would you?" Cookie asked before she realized how it sounded. "I mean, she does push the envelope when it comes to rules, and I know how much you hate that."

Hunter chuckled. "Yes. She sure does." He gazed into Cookie's eyes for a moment. "But I know how much she means to you, and because of that, Rain matters to me too."

Wow. Cookie was seeing a side of Hunter he usually kept hidden. "Agent O'Neil, are you getting soft on me?"

"Of course not," he said.

"I don't know," Cookie teased. "First you buy a Valentine's Day card, and last night you were flirting with Scarlett, and—"

"Jealous?" Hunter asked as they approached the restaurant.

"What?" Cookie frowned. "No." Was that what he was doing last night when he was cozying up to Scarlett? Trying to make her jealous? And here she believed he'd moved on and was trying to be adult about things, she thought and said, "I think it's sweet. Nothing would make me happier than to have two of the people I care most about be together." An evil thought came to her and she quipped, "We could double date."

Hunter didn't give Cookie the satisfaction of a reply right away. Instead he turned into the parking lot of the Salty Dog first, and then said, "I'm not interested in dating Scarlett."

So that's that, thought Cookie. She shouldn't have been surprised Hunter wasn't quite ready to move on, but she wished she could fast forward to the future where she and Hunter could be friends again. As they neared the entrance to the Salty Dog, Cookie noticed a flower vendor with a cart, and it occurred to her that it was for Valentine's Day. *Today.* Her annoyance at Hunter disappeared and she smiled, because that meant she and her red dress had a date with Dylan Creed and his version of a suit tonight. And she preferred what was under that one a lot more than the one she was currently with.

Hunter stepped up to the man selling flowers, and Cookie watched him as he purchased a single red rose. She didn't find out who it was for until they were seated at a table and he handed it to her. "Happy Valentine's Day, Charlie."

She took the flower, careful not to prick her finger on a thorn. There was something significant about a red rose, and Cookie squirmed a little as she wondered if there they were about to have an awkward conversation. Before she could say anything, the waitress appeared holding two small glasses.

"Champagne for the lovers!" exclaimed the perky girl Cookie didn't recognize.

"I—we—" Cookie stammered.

Hunter cut in. "We're just very good friends. And we'll take two everything-but-the-kitchen-sink breakfasts please."

Cookie smiled at him for the relief she felt, as well as the fact he'd just ordered the largest breakfast they made.

Hunter held up his glass of champagne. "Let's toast, Charlie." She lifted her glass too as he said, "We've been through a lot together over the years. You know, I remember the first time I saw you."

"You do?" Cookie thought about the day she met Hunter. She was a rookie assigned to him as his partner, and she wasn't afraid to admit now that he'd scared the daylights out of her.

"When you came through the door, every man in the place watched you walk by," Hunter said. "I wished right then that you were going to be my partner instead of the cocky man child I was sure had been assigned to me. I couldn't believe it when you stuck your hand out and told me *you* were Charlie."

Cookie chuckled as she recalled the way Hunter had raised his eyebrows at her and didn't speak. She also remembered she'd been so nervous she hadn't been able to shut up. "And then once I opened my mouth, you wished you had gotten a guy."

Hunter let out a deep laugh. "No. That is *not* what I was thought."

"No? I think you knew my life story by the time I was done introducing myself."

He shook his head. "Don't be mad at me for this, but I remember thinking it was a shame, because a beautiful woman like you would never last. But you were one surprise after another, Charlie."

Cookie had put up with a lot of flak over the years for being one of the few females in the bureau, and even though Hunter just admitted he'd seen her as a pretty face at first, he'd never treated her like anything less than an equal. "And you never made me feel less than worthy of the job. Thank you for that, because I made a lot of mistakes that first year."

Hunter let out a short laugh. "Remember your Dumpster-diving incident?"

Cookie groaned as she recalled being so eager to catch a perp that she dove right in after him into a mountain of waste from a Chinese restaurant. She'd pulled lo mien noodles out of her hair for days. "Sweet and sour chicken has been forever ruined for me." Her glass clinked when she hit it against his. "But I got the guy."

"You sure did." Hunter and Cookie both took a sip of their champagne, and he gave her a slow smile as they swallowed. "You got this one too."

Dread filled her. Is this where he'd been going this whole time? Why hadn't she seen it more clearly? She cleared her throat, preparing for the inevitable awkward conversation. "Hunter—"

He held up his hand. "It's okay, Charlie. Just let me say this."

She gave him a quick nod.

"I'm always going to love you, and while I know you're in love with Dylan, I don't believe it's forever."

Cookie reached out for his hand as her heart filled with sadness. She loved her former partner, but she wasn't *in* love with him the way she was with Dylan. Maybe if Dylan hadn't come along she and Hunter would have eventually made a go of something. But it wasn't going to happen now. "Hunter, I'm so sorry I've hurt you." Maybe Dylan wouldn't be forever, but keeping Hunter in the wings was wrong on so many levels, and she couldn't let him think otherwise. "Please don't wait for me. It's time for you to move on and find a woman that makes you happier than I ever could."

He shook his head. "That's not possible."

Cookie sighed.

"I'm not going to make you uncomfortable with this," Hunter said.

"Well I sure the hell am," Dylan growled.

Cookie looked up in surprise and her heart stopped beating. She knew how this must look. Champagne, a rose—she yanked her hand away from Hunter. "This—" she glanced at Hunter. "It's not—" and then she noticed everyone in the restaurant was staring at them.

Dylan followed her gaze, grimaced, and speaking in a low voice said, "Let's take this outside."

She jumped up from her chair without a word to Hunter and scrambled to keep up with Dylan's long stride as he moved quickly out of the Salty Dog. Once they were outside Dylan turned to face her, his jaw clenched and fire in his eyes. "Start talking," he said.

"It was just breakfast as friends. We were reminiscing about the past." She stopped to take a breath and collect herself. Telling Dylan that Hunter still had feelings for her wasn't going to go over well, but Cookie knew a relationship needed to be based on trust. A good one, anyway. And she knew Dylan should hear the truth. "Hunter said—" She scowled as she searched for the right words. "Well…"

Dylan let out a noise of disgust. "Champagne brunch on Valentine's Day says it all. He doesn't think of you two as just *friends*."

"In my defense, I didn't know about the champagne. If I had I wouldn't have come."

Dylan's eyebrows shot up into his hairline. "Really?

You would have said no to *Agent O'Neil.*" Cookie didn't like the sarcastic tone in Dylan's voice and anger began to bubble in her veins as he said, "The man is still in love with you, and I think you like it. So much for making a choice."

He wasn't being fair, and Cookie'd had just about enough of both Hunter's and Dylan's jealousy. "It's not like that."

She was gearing up to give Dylan a piece of her mind when the door of the restaurant creaked open. The perky waitress from earlier stepped out carrying a bag and a paper coffee cup and said, "Sir? Your breakfast is ready."

"Thank you," Dylan said as he took the food from the girl.

She smiled sweetly at him. "Have a happy Valentine's Day."

He looked at Cookie. "Right. You too." Then he turned to walk away.

"Dylan!" Cookie watched in amazement as he continued to move as if he hadn't heard her. "Dylan, we're not done here!"

He stopped and turned back to look at her. His expression was cold and his voice just as icy when he said, "Yes, Cookie. We are. At least until you figure out what it is you really want. I'm sure you and Agent O'Neil can handle the investigation without me."

Before she could get another word out, he turned and walked away, taking a piece of Cookie's heart with him.

16.

COOKIE STOOD STARING after Dylan even after he disappeared around the corner. Tears burned the backs of her eyes as she wondered why the tough-FBI-agent side of her was missing in action, because all she wanted to do was curl up in a ball and cry. She was sure Hunter was not who she wanted, but she had to admit that Dylan finding her with him at a Valentine's Day brunch sure didn't make it look that way.

Damn it! She had a mess to clean up, but now wasn't the time.

A chill sent a shiver through her, and she realized she was going to freeze out in the cold February morning. Especially without a coat. Cookie sniffed back her tears and swallowed down her pain before she made her way back into the restaurant.

By the time she got to Hunter, Cookie was back in agent mode. There was a case to solve, and she wasn't about to let her emotions get in the way of doing her job. She sat back down and picked up her fork to dig into the huge breakfast that had been delivered while she was out. "Sorry about that," she said as she dug into a pile of hash browns.

Hunter reached out and grabbed her wrist before she could shove a second bite in her mouth. "Want to talk about it?"

Cookie pulled her hand out of his grasp. "Nope." She stuffed eggs into her mouth and spoke around them. "I'm hungry, and we've got a murder to solve."

"All business now?"

"All business. Got the warrant?"

Hunter nodded, but his expression was one of concern, and Cookie was afraid he wasn't done with the personal. She wasn't about to entertain anymore discussion involving her love life so she said, "Good. Because we need to get our hands on that journal and see if we can find out who Lydia's lover was."

There was nothing like a little drama in Cookie's life to give her an appetite, and when she managed to polish off her entire breakfast she started eyeing the piece of bacon Hunter had left on his plate. She reached over for it, but Hunter slapped at her hand like she was a naughty child.

"Hey!" Cookie exclaimed as she rubbed her stinging skin. "What was that for?"

Hunter grabbed the strip of bacon and shoved it in his mouth as his eyes danced with laughter. "I'm taking one for the team. Now let's get out of here."

After Hunter paid for their meal, they stepped back

SWEET CORPSE OF MINE

outside to make the short walk to Lydia and Blake's house. "I bet Lydia's killer has been in town right under our noses this entire time," Cookie said.

"I bet you're right," Hunter agreed.

"And to think they've been paying to store her dead body for five years." Cookie shook her head. Other than serial killers, murderers usually had a conscience, and Cookie was willing to bet whoever ended Lydia's life wasn't a seasoned criminal who saw her death as a typical job hazard. "How does someone live with that kind of guilt?"

Hunter didn't have a chance to answer Cookie's question because their attention was diverted when a shiny black car sped by, splashing slush up from its wheels.

The black Mustang looked an awful lot like the one Hunter had rented. But Winter was behind the wheel, and in the back seat… "Was that—" Cookie gazed at Hunter in shock. "Please tell me that *wasn't* my mother."

"With Swan's face in her… sequins?" Hunter asked.

"Yeah."

Hunter cocked an eyebrow at Cookie.

"Crap on a cracker." Rain was supposed to get rid of the man, and while it wasn't too farfetched to think she might give him a ride considering his inebriated state, his proximity to her mother was—well. Perhaps Rain did have a thing for Deputy Swan. Cookie shuddered at the thought of Swan hanging out at the inn and the things he would do with—"Arg!" she cried out as she squeezed her eyes shut, hoping to stop the images from searing her mind.

"Maybe it's not what it looked like," Hunter offered.

"Maybe." Cookie wanted to believe Hunter. More than she could possibly express with words. But she knew her mother. One of Rain's best qualities was her ability to see the good in anyone, even a man like Deputy Swan. Though, she certainly hadn't liked him much before. When had things changed?

Cookie thought about how she hadn't seen Hale, or even heard much lately about the man who was Rain's main squeeze. Maybe things had cooled off between them and Cookie hadn't noticed. She racked her brain trying to remember if Rain had mentioned anything about a break up but then shook her head. If Rain and Hale were no longer a thing, surely she'd have known. Right?

The vision of Swan and her mother kissing—it made her shudder. And then she mentally chastised herself. Cookie kicked at a piece of ice, and pain radiated through her toe as it skittered across the street. Who was she to judge who people fell in love with? It wasn't too long ago Cookie was struggling with her own feelings for two men in her life, all the while knowing she was causing both of them pain as she took the time she needed to make a decision. And now the one she picked didn't believe she'd fully committed herself to him.

Cookie let out a sigh.

This was one confusing Valentine's Day. It was as if

Cupid's aim was off, and it made Cookie want to forget the holiday existed. Fortunately, she had the distraction of a case. She pointed to the street sign that read 'Church Street' and said, "Blake and Lydia's house should be on the left."

Church Street was one of the oldest streets in town, and the homes had been mansions in their day. They walked by Colonial-style houses with columns, wrap-around porches, and widow's walks until they came to the Rosen's home. A couple of plastic-wrapped newspapers were on the stoop and it occurred to Cookie that Blake couldn't call a neighbor to gather the mail when he was in jail.

"Where did Blake say the key is?" Hunter asked.

After they'd gotten consent to search Blake house, he'd willingly informed them of where to find the spare key. "In the iron lobster next to the door."

As Hunter retrieved the key and worked the lock, Cookie emptied the mailbox. Hunter scowled at her. "You've lived on this island too long if you're now collecting suspects' mail for them."

Cookie shrugged. It was true she wouldn't have done such a thing in Philly, but life on Secret Seal Isle was different. The pace moved slowly and it was as if time did too, because people still looked out for each other. And she liked it. It felt right to get Blake's mail, no matter what kind of trouble he was in. But she wasn't sure she could explain it to Hunter, so she began to shuffle through the envelopes and flyers. As paper rustled she said, "I'm just checking for clues."

They stepped into an open entryway that rose up two of the three stories of the house. Off to the right was a parlor and to the left a sitting room with a TV. Cookie said, "Winter found the diary in a box on the desk of Lydia's study."

An Oriental carpet muffled their footsteps as they walked down a hall and saw a formal dining room on the left. Further down on the right they found a study, and because it was decorated in shades of burgundy and pink, the feminine appearance made them think it had to have been Lydia's room. Hunter and Cookie stepped inside, and Hunter pointed to what appeared to be a hand-carved box on top of the desk. "That must be it."

Cookie sat herself in the antique chair to open the drawer of the desk in search of the key. It was on top of a box of stationery, and the metal was slick in her fingers as she took it to open the box. Sure enough, a brown, leather-bound journal was inside.

The diary was thick, and when Cookie opened the book they discovered it was nearly full of handwriting as well as ticket stubs from a Broadway show, a concert, and a flower show. "This could take a while," she said as she flipped through the pages. Cookie stopped when she found a receipt tucked between two pages, and she removed it to inspect more closely. It was for a journal from the stationery store where Cookie had bought Dylan's card. When she flipped it over, she saw a series of numbers on the back. "Wait a minute."

Hunter peered over her shoulder and said, "That looks like a phone number." He pulled out his cell. "Let's see who it belongs to."

As he held the phone to his ear he broke into a grin. "Voicemail."

Cookie smiled too, because that meant they'd get a name without having to explain why they'd called. As he listened, she skimmed the page of the diary that the receipt had marked, and a section caught her eye. *I met a man today I can't stop thinking about. I don't know what to do.*

"It's Andrew DePaul's number," Hunter said.

"That's the guy who owns the stationery shop," Cookie said. "Huh. Listen to this." She read the lines Lydia had written about meeting a guy. While the receipt could have just been marking a place in the journal, Cookie had a feeling it was connected to the man Lydia had met. And it could very well be one gift shop owner named Andrew DePaul. "It looks like we need to go see Andy again."

17.

THE BELL OF the stationery shop let out a cheerful ring when Cookie and Hunter walked through the door to see Andy, but for a split he looked anything but happy when he saw them. Cookie attributed it to the fact that Valentine's Day was likely a busy time as significant others scrambled to get their lovers a gift at the last minute.

"Andy!" Cookie exclaimed. "You look much better than the last time we were here."

"Yes," he said as he gave her a smile of his own. The cash drawer rattled when it opened as he finished ringing up the only other customer in the store. He handed a bag to the man. "Thank you, Roger. Have a great evening."

"You too," the man said, and he offered Hunter and Cookie a nod before he left.

Andy came out from behind the counter. "I must have eaten something that didn't agree with me, because I feel much better now."

"I'm glad to hear it," Cookie said. She turned to

Hunter. "Agent O'Neil and I would like to ask you a few questions about our current investigation."

Andy sighed. "I heard about Lydia Rosen. So tragic."

Hunter said, "It is. But Ms. James and I have every intention of seeing that justice is served."

"Of course," Andy said. "How can I help?"

"How well did you know Lydia?" Cookie asked.

Andy shook his head. "Barely at all. I think we only ran into each other a couple of times."

"I'm sure this is a busy day for you so we'll be brief." Hunter pulled out the receipt they'd found and showed it to Andy. "This was in Lydia Rosen's diary, and as you can see, the number on the back is yours."

Andy frowned for a moment. "That is very odd. I certainly didn't know the woman well enough to give her my number." His expression suddenly changed and he said, "Ohhhh. I remember now. The day Lydia came here to buy the journal she was with Julie Taylor." He gave them a sheepish grin. "I remember that very well, because I gave Julie my number and we dated for a while. I don't understand why Lydia would've kept it, though."

"Yes. That is strange," Cookie said. But she had an idea of how the receipt might have gotten in Lydia's diary. Considering Julie had spent a good deal of time trying to comfort Blake over Lydia's disappearance, it wouldn't be a stretch to think she'd visited Blake's home. That meant Julie would have had ample opportunity to plant the evidence if she was trying to frame Andy. But why would she?

The bell to the front door rang again as a harried-looking man entered. Andy merely pointed in the direction of the Valentine's Day cards and said, "There's candy the next aisle over too."

The man waved his hand at Andy as he rushed over to get his gift. Cookie glanced at Hunter who dropped his chin as a signal he had no further questions. She said, "Thank you so much for your time, Andy. We'll let you get back to work."

"You're welcome. Good luck with the investigation."

Once Hunter and Cookie were outside, they headed toward the historical society building. Cookie said, "I'm not sure what to think."

"You like Andy for this?" asked Hunter.

"I'm not ruling him out completely, but I'm leaning toward Julie. She could have planted the evidence at Blake's house to frame Andy and cover up what she did."

"Or what Blake did," Hunter said. "Look, Charlie. I know you want him to be innocent, but we still don't know that he is."

"I'm aware," she said with a bit of annoyance in her voice. Icy wind blew a strand of hair in her face, and she swiped it out of the way with a mittened hand. Cookie knew she was relying too heavily on her gut, but she really believed Blake wasn't Lydia's killer. She supposed that was why she and Hunter worked so well together. Whenever one of them blindly trusted their intuition, the other would keep them grounded in the facts. "Sorry," she said. "I know you're just keeping me honest, Hunter."

"You do the same for me," he said. They'd reached the historical society and Hunter stopped walking. He tugged on the bottom of his jacket and straightened his tie as if he were about to pick up a date for the first time.

Cookie chuckled at him, and he cocked an eyebrow at her as if to ask, *What?*

"No breath spray?" she asked. "C'mon lover boy, let's go give Julie her valentine."

Apparently the historical society was not a hot spot for Valentine's Day, because they entered into a nearly empty building. And Julie was on them like flies on honey the moment they did. Correction. She was on *Hunter* the moment they walked in.

"Agent O'Neil," Julie cooed. "What a lovely surprise. Today of all days." She placed a hand on her chest above her left breast. "Be still my beating heart."

Cookie choked back a laugh as Hunter flirted right back with an amused smile. "Ms. Taylor, it's nice to see you again too."

"Julie. Please." The woman giggled while Cookie tried not to gag. "To what do I owe the pleasure?"

"We have a few more questions to ask you about our investigation," Cookie said.

"Oh." Julie's expression turned hard as she looked at Cookie. "I'm not sure what else I can possibly tell you."

Hunter reached in his jacket and pulled out the receipt. "We found something in Lydia's journal that is interesting." He held out the piece of paper. "It seems she was using this as a bookmark, but oddly Andy

DePaul's number is on the back. When we asked Andy about it, he said he gave it to you."

Julie took the receipt from Hunter and read the number. "Yes. This is Drew's number, but he never gave this to me."

Drew? "So he never gave you his number?" Cookie asked.

"I didn't say that."

"Did you two have a relationship?" asked Hunter.

Drew, Cookie thought again and frowned as she tried to determine what was significant about the nickname.

Julie smiled at Hunter. "We did. But it was *years* ago, and our relationship was very short lived."

"I see," Hunter said.

"Drew and I spent time together working a fundraiser for the town through the Chamber of Commerce," Lydia said. "You know those cute little ducks we float down the river each spring?" Hunter nodded as she went on. "Well. Drew and I got along and—" Julie's voice faded in the background as Cookie latched onto why the name Drew was rolling around in her head. *Drew DePaul fit the initials D.D.!*

Suddenly Cookie didn't think Andy was sick the other day. At least not from something he ate, because Drew DePaul could have been Lydia's lover. The pieces began to fall into place, but Cookie knew she didn't have time to tie this up in a neat bow. If it was Andy, he knew they were dangerously close to discovering the truth, and he could be packing up his car to skip town as they spoke.

She grabbed Hunter's arm and interrupted Julie. "Excuse me. Thank you, but we have everything we need for today."

"We do?" Hunter asked, pinching his eyebrows together as he studied her.

"We do," Cookie confirmed and tugged Hunter toward the door.

"You don't want to hear about the time Drew tried to kiss me and I kneed him in the junk?" Julie asked, her eyes glinting with mischief.

Hunter grimaced, but still turned to her with interest. "You did? Why?"

"He was getting fresh," she said primly.

"Okay. Maybe we can get the details later," Cookie said. "Right now we have somewhere to be. Thanks, Julie."

"Um, sure." The woman slid up to Hunter and ran a hand down his lapel. "I'm not sure I was helpful, but if you need anything else, my door is always open."

"Uh." Hunter cast Cookie a desperate look, clearly asking her to rescue him.

Cookie rolled her eyes. "I'm sure Agent O'Neill will remember that, Julie. Thanks again." She tightened her hold on his arm and dragged him out the front door.

"What was that about?" Hunter asked her the moment they were on the sidewalk.

"What? You mean the part about Julie throwing herself at you, and you getting caught like a deer in the headlights?" she asked, leading the way down Main Street to Deputy Swan's office. Hopefully Rain had been giving him a lift back to work and the two weren't off doing—Cookie didn't even want to think about it. They were going to need an arrest warrant before they could go after Drew, and if Swan wasn't around, she'd call Rain to find out where he was hiding. "You'd think you never had to turn down an aggressive witness before."

He gave her a flat stare. "Not that. And I wasn't caught like a deer in the headlights. I was distracted by your sudden ninety-degree shift. Julie said something to trigger that brain of yours, didn't she?'

"Yes, while you were flirting, I was thinking," Cookie said, giving him a smirk.

It was his turn to roll his eyes. "Okay, out with it."

"Drew DePaul. Do the initials D.D. ring a bell?"

Hunter's eyes narrowed, then his lips curved into a satisfied smile. "You think Andrew DePaul gave Lydia that locket."

"Exactly. And we need to get a warrant and arrest him before he leaves town. After our questioning today, how much you want to bet he's already packing a bag?"

He snorted. "I know better than to bet against your hunches." Hunter quickened his pace and glanced over at her. "Keep up, Charlie. We have a case to put to bed."

HUNTER HELD THE door open to the small Sheriff's office. Cookie quickly strode in and headed for the enclosed glass office in the far right corner. She could see the back of Swan's head lolling to the side in the office chair. Cripes. Was he passed out? She couldn't tell. The chair was turned around, facing the wall. The only thing she knew for sure was that Swan wasn't moving.

"Deputy Swan," Cookie called as she stepped through the door.

Nothing. He didn't move.

"Swan!" Cookie rounded the chair, irritation making her grit her teeth. She reached for him, grabbing and shaking his arm, but instead of jolting awake, the deputy slid sideways, lying limp in the chair.

"Damn." Hunter muttered and reached for Swan's pulse. He raised his gaze to Cookie's and shook his head. "Swan's dead."

"But…" Cookie frowned and glanced at the time on her phone. "How is that possible? We just saw him with my mother, oh, thirty-five minutes ago."

Hunter let out another curse.

Cookie's body tensed. "What is it?"

"Swan's body is too cold." His jaw tensed as a pained expression flashed over his handsome features. "There's no way this man just died."

Suddenly Cookie's stomach felt like her breakfast had contained the kitchen sink. "Oh, Rain," Cookie whispered. "What did you do?"

Hunter sighed. "Call your mother. Make sure there isn't anything we need to know before I call Watkins."

Dread ate at Cookie's insides as her blood ran cold. If

there had been any foul play—she shook her head violently and reached into her pocket, fumbling for her phone.

Her mother answered on the first ring. "Cookie!" She let out a nervous giggle. "How's the investigation going? Are you and Hunter going to call it a day soon? I thought you had plans with Dylan tonight. I'm sure me and Scarlett can entertain Hunter until I leave to show off my present to Hale. I got him—"

"Mother," Cookie cut off her rambling. "Where are you?"

"At the inn. Where else would I be, dear?"

"Oh, I don't know, tooling around in the Mustang after dropping Swan off at the sherriff's office."

Silence. There wasn't even any background noise from the inn. Cookie pulled the phone away from her ear and glanced at the screen. The call was still connected.

"Mom, is there something you need to tell me?" Cookie asked, a warning in her tone.

"Um, nooooo," Rain said with a whine.

Cookie closed her eyes and sighed deeply. "What happened? And don't lie to me."

"It wasn't my fault. I swear! I was doing a naughty little dance, pretending like I was going to strip down to a black satin teddy. But I totally wasn't going to show him any of the goods! I mean, Hale wouldn't go for that, and I'm not that kind of girl. But when I started unbuttoning my shirt and flashed him just a smidge of cleavage, suddenly he was clutching at his chest. At first, I thought he was just a little overwhelmed. Because you know, I am pretty sexy. Any man might have a trouble resisting this. Right?"

Cookie was gripping the phone so tightly she half expected the protective case to crack. "Mom, I don't need the exposition. Just tell me what happened next."

"You needed to get the full picture so you know it's not my fault. I swear I didn't know my sexual prowess was going to be his downfall. It's not like I've ever killed a man with just a little flash of flesh before, now have I?"

"Not that I'm aware of," Cookie admitted.

"See? I couldn't have known. Anyway, I continued to tease him by undoing another button, and the next thing I knew, he was gasping for air as his face turned gray. Then he just fell over, dead, right there in the office. I tried CPR and mouth to mouth. I swear I tried, Cookie. He was just… he was gone."

"And you didn't think to call 911?"

"Of course I did. But you know how long it would take for an ambulance to get here. By the time they got across the ferry, there was no way he was going to survive. And I happen to know Doctor Charming is down in Florida getting his flirt on. There was no one to call."

Doctor Charming was the eighty-year-old retired doctor who, as long as he was on the island, could usually be counted on to help in an emergency. "So you put him in the car and took him to the sheriff's office?"

Cookie asked, incredulously.

"I couldn't risk anyone knowing he was here, now could I? What would Hale say? Plus, I didn't want to get busted for obstruction of justice. You won't tell Hunter, will you? I know that man has been dying to put me in handcuffs for years."

"For the love of…" Cookie ran a hand through her hair. "I can't believe you did this." But of course she could believe it. Why wouldn't she? Rain wasn't exactly the most rational person who ever lived, even if her intentions were honorable.

"He just…" Rain let out a small sob. "I didn't mean to kill him. It's all my fault. If I didn't have such a rockin' body, he'd still be here."

A vision of her mother in her sagging leather pants crossed her mind, and Cookie had to fight to not chuckle at her mother's conclusion. Leave it to Rain to be absurd in the most inappropriate situations. Cookie cleared her throat. "Calm down, Mom. It's not your fault he had a weak heart. Just… stay home and don't say anything about this to anyone. Got it?"

"Winter knows."

Of course she did. She'd been driving the Mustang and no doubt had helped Rain move the body. "Just tell her to keep it to herself. Tell no one else. Not even Scarlett. Got it?"

"You want me to keep secrets from Scarlett?" Her mother tsked. "Since when do we do that?"

"Plausible deniability," Cookie said, rubbing her

forehead. "This is to protect her, not shut her out."

"Am I... Oh my god. Am I in trouble?"

"Only if someone finds out. Listen, Mom. I have to go. Stay home. Don't get into any more trouble. Got it?"

"Yes." Her mother's voice was distant, contrite. "Hurry back, okay? Today was... rough."

Cookie softened her tone. "I'll be there as soon as I can." She pressed the End button and glanced up to see Hunter staring at her. "He had a heart attack in my office. Rain and Winter, in their infinite wisdom, thought it would be bad if he was found there."

A muscle in Hunter's neck bulged as he fought to control his anger. Cookie was acutely aware she'd just asked, without actually asking, an FBI agent to overlook a crime. Without saying a word, he pressed a button on his phone and turned his back to her.

Cookie walked out of the glass office and paced. Swan was dead. Her mother was a criminal. Dylan wasn't speaking to her. But right then they needed to focus on apprehending Drew before he skipped town. She was absolutely certain he was Lydia's lover, and that put him right at the top of the suspect list.

As annoyed as she was at her mother for overreacting and getting herself into trouble, Cookie was also worried about her. She'd sounded scared and emotionally drained when Cookie had ended the call. The desire to run home and make sure Rain was all right pulled at her heart. But she couldn't go. She had a job to do. A murderer to apprehend. Still, there was someone she could call who'd keep an eye on Rain, no questions asked.

Cookie pulled her phone out and dialed Scarlett.

"Cookie, happy Valentine's Day! Are you excited for your hot date with Dylan tonight?"

"Hey, Scar," Cookie said with a smile. "Happy Valentine's Day, yourself. Got any hot plans of your own?"

Scarlett scoffed. "Not unless you count a little banter with Larry down at the Salty Dog. I thought I'd grab something to eat later while the rest of you are out sexing up your boy-toys."

"Sounds better than watching romantic tragedies and eating your weight in chocolates," Cookie said through a smile.

"No doubt." Scarlett chuckled. "The last time we did that, we also chugged the vodka and took turns holding each other's hair back. I think I'll pass."

"Definitely." Cookie walked to the front door and stared out at the snowy street. "Listen, Scar. I need you to do something for me."

"Sure. Anything."

"Can you keep an eye on my mother this afternoon? She's had… an eventful morning. I've asked her to lay low at the inn until I can get back there, but you know Rain. Sometimes she's a little…"

"Impulsive? Flighty? A pain in the butt?"

Cookie laughed. "All of the above."

"What happened?" Scarlett asked.

"You really don't want to know. Not right now.

Trust me on this one."

Scarlett let out a low whistle. "Sounds juicy. You'll fill me in later?"

"No doubt, but for right now, it's best to let it lie," Cookie said.

"Gotcha. No problem. I've been out on the other side of the island taking pictures. I'll head back now and keep her chained to the inn."

"Thanks. I appreciate it."

"I know," Scarlett said and ended the call.

Five minutes later, Hunter emerged from Swan's office holding a sheet of fax paper. He held it up, showing off the warrant they needed. "Let's go."

Cookie glanced back at the office. "What about Swan?"

"He's not going anywhere."

18.

COOKIE HAD TO run to keep up with Hunter. The cold air stung her face, numbing her nose. But she could practically see steam radiating from Hunter. He was angry. Angrier than usual. The tension in his neck and his clipped, jerky movements as he trudged down Main Street were a dead giveaway.

"Hunter! Wait up," Cookie called after him, jogging to catch up. He'd always been a fast walker, but usually that wasn't an issue for her. She was tall and had an impressive stride herself. But today, he was giving her a run for her money.

"Why?" he snapped back as he came to an abrupt stop and rounded on her. "The only thing I get here on this island is a load of crap. You couldn't just leave me alone, could you? Now I have to watch you with some other guy while your mother once again puts my career in jeopardy. Christ, Charlie. Can you think of any reason why I should be here?"

Cookie gulped, her face burning with embarrassment

and her heart cracking from the pain she hadn't intended to cause him. "Because it's your job to catch the bad guys?"

He snorted divisively. "There are other agents who can handle this small town BS."

She reared back, feeling as if he'd punched her in the gut. This was the seventh case Hunter had helped her with since she'd moved to the out of the way island. And while the cases hadn't dealt with career mobsters or the cartel, they had brought down a couple of international art thieves and drug dealers. They'd done important work and had saved lives, made a real difference for the locals. Still, she couldn't argue with his assessment. There were other agents or law enforcement officers who could handle the cases. She just hadn't been able to entertain that possibility.

Hunter had been her partner for the better part of a decade. Moving, changing her life, starting a relationship with Dylan, all of those things were changes she'd wanted and knew in her heart were the right moves. But losing her partner, the person she trusted to have her back on every mission, left a Hunter-shaped hole in her heart.

"You're right. You don't have to be the one to do any of this," she said thickly. "I shouldn't have called. I chose this life, this town. You didn't. I just…" She shook her head and shrugged as she lifted her hands, palms up. "You were my partner. And you're who I do this with."

Hunter's dark gaze bored into hers. There was war

raging in those dark eyes of his. An internal, private war she knew she shouldn't be privy to. She just knew him too well. Just like her knew her... or used to anyway. Cookie realized she'd changed since moving to the island. Her plans, her goals, what she wanted out of life were all different now. Still, she was the same Charlie Jamieson on the inside that she'd always been. And the FBI agent lying dormant inside of her sprang to life. There was no time for fights or regrets or forgiveness. Right then, they had a perp to catch.

"Come on," she said, giving him an out. He didn't need to say anything. Not then, maybe not ever. He owed her nothing. Not anymore. She'd made her choices and he needed to make his. "We need to catch up with Drew before it's too late."

Hunter blew out a long breath and grasped the back of his neck with one hand. "Right. You think he's still at the store?"

Relief fluttered through her chest. It was always the same with them. No matter what was going on, they each had the capacity to shove it aside and get the job done. She pasted on a smile. "Seems like the best place to start."

"Then let's go." Hunter turned and once again strode down the street. Only this time, his movements were graceful and smooth, the previously obvious agitation gone.

Cookie fell into step beside him, easily keeping up with his clipped pace.

"If for some reason he's not there, any ideas on where to look next? Besides the ferry I mean?" Hunter asked. "Do you know this guy at all?"

"Not really," Cookie admitted. "If he's not at his shop or his apartment, the next logical step is to make sure he hasn't hopped the ferry. After that, I guess we just start canvassing the island."

"Let's do this," said Hunter.

A few minutes later, they came to a stop in front of Drew's shop. The lights were off and the sign read Closed. The hours posted indicated the shop was open from 9 to 4 Tuesday through Sunday. It was Monday, and Drew must have only opened in the morning for the holiday. This couldn't be easy, Cookie thought. If she hadn't been dealing with her mother's explanation of her criminal behavior or fighting with Hunter, it was likely they'd have arrived in time before Drew closed up shop.

Cookie scowled and cupped her hands around her eyes as she peered through the glass.

"I think it's safe to say he isn't in there," Hunter said.

"You don't know that," Cookie said. "He could be closing out his register in the back or doing inventory or something."

Hunter raised a skeptical eyebrow. "You think he'd take time to do paperwork if he's planning to run for it?"

"No," she said, irritated he was right. Even with a run on Valentine's Day cards and heart-shaped boxes of candy, it was unlikely Drew brought in enough money to even cover rent of the building. He had to own it outright or have some sort of money stashed away. Selling stationery was a dying business. And to run a store like that on a small island, it was a ludicrous to think it was profitable enough he'd risk getting apprehended just to make a mediocre bank deposit.

Cookie moved to the left and hit a button next to the unmarked door that she assumed would lead to an apartment above.

Nothing happened.

She pressed it again, holding it down, hoping the buzzer was loud and annoying enough that it would drive Drew to buzz them in.

"Who are you looking for?" a woman asked from behind Cookie.

Cookie spun, spotting a cute, dark-haired woman in her early twenties, holding a dozen long-stemmed roses. Her cheeks were flushed, her red lipstick was smudged, and her brilliant blue eyes sparkled. She was glowing with love and happiness. Someone had made her Valentine's Day one to remember. "Andy DePaul. Do you know him?"

"Sure. He's my neighbor. Kind of a recluse though. Once he closes up shop for the night, he sort of disappears into his apartment and doesn't reemerge until the next day. He never opens the door for anyone."

Hunter moved forward, his FBI badge in his hand. "It's imperative that we speak with him. Do you think you can help us out and let us in this door?"

The young woman glanced from the badge to

Hunter's face, then back to mine. "FBI? Is Andy in some sort of trouble?"

"That's not something we're at liberty to discuss," Hunter said, all business. "But it would be a great help if you could unlock that door."

"I don't—" the girl started.

Cookie placed a light hand on her arm. "Please. It's imperative that we talk to Andy as soon as possible." Cookie didn't want to frighten the woman and tell her that Andy, her neighbor, was a suspected murderer, but she would if she had to in order to get through that door.

The woman nodded and let out a heavy sigh. "Okay, but don't tell him it was me. He'll get really angry, and I can't afford to live anywhere else right now."

He was her landlord. That explained a lot about how he was able to stay in business. "Wouldn't dream of mentioning it," Cookie said.

The brunette nodded once, inserted her key, and pulled the door open. "I'm going to go up first. Can you wait just a minute before following me?"

Hunter was practically vibrating with tension and impatience. Cookie knew the feeling. They didn't have precious minutes to waste.

"Sorry," Cookie said, her hand already reaching for the weapon tucked in her jeans at the small of her back. "This is urgent."

Hunter swept past them both and entered the hall, his weapon pointed to the floor as he cleared the area. The young woman let out a high-pitched gasp and turned to Cookie with wild eyes. So much for not scaring her.

"It'll be all right. Just a precaution," Cookie said, giving her a warm smile. Andy hadn't given them any reason to suspect he was violent. Well, nothing other than strangling Lydia, but the space was enclosed, with nowhere to take cover or escape. In their line of work, they had to be cautious. Not just for their own safety, but for the safety of those around them.

The young woman shook her head and backed away, texting one handed on her phone.

Aw, crap. Cookie took two quick steps forward and grabbed her by the shoulder. "Listen. It's better if you go to a friend's—" Cookie cut her gaze to the flowers still clutched in the woman's hands "—or a boyfriend's house while we do what we need to do. But please don't spread this around. We don't need gawkers getting in the line of fire."

Another gasp and one single tear fell down her right cheek.

Double crap! Cookie cursed herself. She was failing at keeping this girl calm. "Just go, okay? Everything will be—"

"Charlie, get in here," Hunter's deep voice called from the top of the stairs.

"Just go," Cookie said one more time, giving the girl a gentle nudge in the direction she'd come from. Then she spun on her heel and sprinted up the stairs. To the right were two doors. One said Manager and was wide open. The other just had a faded number 1 smack in the middle.

Hunter pointed his gun at the manager's apartment. "It must be that one."

"Have you cleared it yet?" Cookie asked, already knowing the answer was no. He wouldn't do it by himself if he didn't have to. Backup was always safer.

He shook his head.

Cookie nodded and flattened herself against the wall beside the door, holding her gun, pointed up, with both hands. Their eyes met for the briefest second then Hunter nodded. Cookie spun, pointing her gun into the apartment, careful to keep close to the right wall. The place looked like it had gone through a tornado or been tossed. A chair was overturned, and Cookie had to avoid stepping on broken glass from a lamp as she walked by.

Hunter followed her, covering her left side, moving toward the opening to what appeared to be the kitchen. "Clear," he called.

Cookie kicked the bedroom door open and scanned the room, her gun still aimed in front of her. She checked the closet and yelled, "Clear."

She heard Hunter stride across the apartment. A door banged open. A second later, he confirmed the bathroom was clear as well. Cookie joined him in the living room. Andy wasn't home.

"Robbery?" Cookie asked, scanning the contents of the room.

"If so, they came for something specific. And they

had access. No forced entry. Electronics haven't been touched. Neither have the video games." He nodded his head to the bar area separating the kitchen and living room. "There's a computer over there."

"The bedroom isn't trashed," Cookie added as she peered into the room again. "There's even some cash on the dresser. Abducted?"

Hunter shrugged. "No real sign of a struggle."

Sure the place was a mess, but it looked more like someone had gone into a fit of rage and thrown anything within reaching distance. Both of the lamps were shattered, as well as a mug and a decorative bowl. The desk had been overturned, and when Cookie snapped on gloves and righted it she discovered a wooden box similar to the one Lydia had owned. It was broken as if someone had taken a hammer to it. Or perhaps the coffee mug. Cookie kneeled down to comb through the debris. The box contained a stack of stationery, and when she looked closely at the top sheet, she discovered it had the imprint of what had been written on top of it.

"Hunter! I think I found something."

Her former partner came out of the kitchen to see as Cookie grabbed a pencil and began to slide it back and forth across the stack of paper to highlight the imprinted text.

It read, 'My darling, Lydia.' As Cookie continued to read she realized it was a love letter with a mix of apologies and regrets over what Drew had done.

"Whoa." Cookie said, and she gathered them into a

pile. "Talk about an evidence payload. While it's not admissible, we've got ourselves a confession right here."

Hunter said, "He sure makes it easy."

Cookie nodded her agreement. Andy was drowning in a cesspool of guilt. All they had to do was catch him, and she was willing to bet he'd crack with the first round of questioning. The ones who felt remorse were the ones most likely to confess.

Hunter disappeared into the bedroom. Cookie heard the screech of dresser drawers opening, followed by what must have been the closet door slamming against the wall. Hunter ran back into the living room, and didn't slow down as he yelled, "We've got to go! He's on the run."

Cookie glanced once again into the bedroom and instantly noted the empty dresser drawers Hunter had left open. "Son of a..." She pulled out her phone and called the ferry terminal office over in Hancock. A woman answered on the first ring. "Maine Line Water Transport, Lily speaking. How can I help you today?"

"Hi Lily," she said as her feet pounded down the steps of the apartment building. "This is Cookie James from Secret Seal Isle. Can you patch me through to Captain Bob on the Secret Seal Isle ferry? It's an emergency."

"Captain Bob is down at the local pub getting some dinner. Can I take a message?"

"What do you mean? If he's at the pub, who's running the ferry?"

"No one. It broke down just before lunchtime. It's been out of service since then."

Cookie let out a relieved sigh. "So there's been no ferry service at all this afternoon? No way to get on or off the island?"

"Not unless someone used a private boat. Did you need to leave a message, Ms. James?"

"No. Thank you." Cookie ended the call and grinned at Hunter. She knew from talking to Andy at the chamber meeting he didn't own a boat. She filled Hunter in on the details of her call. "Unless he stole a boat, Andy is somewhere on this island."

"That's something at least," Hunter said. "Let's head to the marina and see if any boats are missing."

19.

A S IT TURNED out, the manager down at the marina informed them that no personal boats had come in or out of the marina all day. There was a small craft advisory, and even the fishermen had called it quits late morning. If Andy had secured a boat, he'd managed to do it without anyone noticing. Which, admittedly, would be difficult to pull off in this nosy town.

"What's still open on the island?" Hunter asked. "Which businesses?"

Cookie glanced at her watch. "Pretty much all of them. Why don't we just start at one end of town and work our way down to the Tipsy Seagull?"

"Or you could get your mother to call around and see if anyone has seen him," Hunter said.

Cookie smiled slowly. "Genius." Rain had become an integral part of the gossip tree on the island. When she put the call out, if anyone had seen him, they'd know about it in minutes. Cookie didn't hesitate.

"Cookie! What's going on?" her mother asked.

"Where are you? You know you have a date with Dylan tonight right?"

"Oh for the love of… of course I remember. Never mind that. Right now I need your help," Cookie said.

"Help? Of course." Rain's tone turned all business. "Anything you need, dear."

"We're looking for Andy DePaul. He's somewhere on the island. Can you make some calls and find out if anyone's seen him in the last hour or so?"

"Absolutely. I'm on it."

Cookie could practically hear Rain bouncing in her seat. "As soon as you hear anything, call me back ASAP. Got it?"

"Will do."

The line went dead, and without hesitation Cookie called Dylan. Voicemail. She hated to admit it, but she was sort of relieved. She knew he was still mad at her, and he had every right to be. She fully intended to make things right, but she wanted to do that in person, not over the phone. Still, he needed to know she might be late for their date… if he was still planning on spending the evening with her.

"Dylan, hi. It's Cookie," she said lamely, as if he wouldn't recognize her voice. "Hunter and I are engaged in a manhunt, searching for Andy DePaul. We've pinpointed him as the prime suspect in Lydia's murder, and he's on the run. But we have reason to believe he's still on the island. We'll be out searching until we find him and bring him in. I wanted—"

Cookie's heart felt as if it were being squeezed by a vice as she recalled the fight she'd had with Dylan earlier. He'd walked away, and she knew he might very well believe their date was off. But she refused to admit it to herself and said, "I needed to let you know I'm not standing you up. No matter how late it is when Hunter and I finish, I want to see you for Valentine's Day." Oh god, what if he really was done with her? She added, "As long as that's okay with you." Cookie took a deep breath, hating the tightness in her chest. "Call me back and let me know if it's not. Otherwise, I'll see you later."

She ended the call and pushed back her emotions before she turned to Hunter. "Let's go."

The two of them checked everyplace they could find from one end of town to the other, ending at the Tipsy Seagull. Valentine's Day certainly made people crazy in this town. They'd narrowly escaped a two-for-one valentine waxing at the Clip, Dip, and Rip. And just now they had to refuse two flaming pink shots called Cupid's Arrow from the insistent bartender who ended up drinking them himself. Cookie was still sorting out how his beard didn't catch fire.

"That was major *heartburn* in a glass if I ever saw it," Hunter said as they stepped outside.

Cookie rolled her eyes at him and said, "That's it for Main Street. We could drive to the other side of the island, but everything over there is going to require us knocking on doors."

Hunter groaned. "Where are the rookies when you

need them? Or beat cops? Did I ever mention how much I hate small towns?"

Cookie felt the same way at that moment. It would be nice to have men staked out at the docks watching boat traffic and to have a few teams going door-to-door. She pulled out her phone for the next best thing to canvassing neighborhoods—Rain.

"Hey, sweetie," her mother said. "I just got off the phone with Peaches." Rain's tone turned serious. "You know, you and Hunter really should have taken her up on the two-for-one. I'd bet my bottom dollar your garden is overgrown." Rain let out a sigh. "And I know you've got a hot date later."

"Gee, thanks, Mom." Cookie took a moment to consider the last time she'd shaved her legs. She winced, having no real idea. Hopefully she'd find fifteen minutes before the date to rectify the situation, assuming Dylan was still interested. "I've got more important things on my mind. Like Lydia's killer and getting Blake out of jail."

"Of course, dear."

When Rain offered no more, Cookie asked, "What did you find out?"

"Dead end I'm afraid. The closest I got was Minnie's husband buying her those cheap chocolates from Andy's shop this morning. And boy did Minnie give me an earful about it. Paul's not getting his annual Valentine's—"

"Mother!" Cookie took a deep breath. She already

knew far too much about the state of many island residents' sex lives thanks to her mother's spot on the grapevine. "I'm sure it's tragic that Paul couldn't have—" *What am I saying?* "Thank you for trying, Mom, and if you hear anything please call me right away."

"I will. We'll catch him. I'm sure of it."

"Yes," Cookie smiled at Rain's use of the word we, because if she could pin a deputy badge on Rain, her mother would wear it proudly. "Thanks, Mom."

Hunter raised an eyebrow at Cookie and she said, "She got nothing." He opened his mouth to say something, but then his phone buzzed. Holding up his index finger, he answered the call.

Cookie took the moment to check her phone as she thought about Dylan. He hadn't called or texted her back. Was he really that mad at her? Her stomach formed a dull ache and she pressed a hand to her abdomen to stop it.

"Ferndale, what can I do for you?" Hunter said into the phone.

Cookie tried not to listen in on what was clearly another FBI agent calling to consult on a case. She turned away and ran through all the various places Andy could be hiding. It was too cold to not be holed-up somewhere. He wasn't at any of the businesses. If they ferry opened while they were canvassing, they could very well lose him. They'd have to have someone over in Hancock monitoring the ferry arrivals.

"Thanks, you've been a great help." Hunter ended

the call and turned to Cookie, smiling conspiratorially. "Ready to return to the scene of the crime?"

She raised one eyebrow. "You mean Sunfish Storage?"

"The one and only. Agent Ferndale just called to let me know he and his partner just apprehended a suspect in the exact spot where his first victim was murdered. Wouldn't be the first time a suspect couldn't stay away. It won't be the last either."

Cookie got where he was going. Considering the storage unit at Sunfish Storage was once a love nest and contained evidence it had also been used as a shrine, it wouldn't be a stretch to think Drew had returned to the scene of his crime either. Cookie kicked herself that they hadn't thought of it earlier. Cookie's lips split into a grin matching Hunter's. "What are we waiting for?"

20.

I T WAS LATE afternoon when Cookie and Hunter arrived at Sunfish Storage, and it was no great surprise they found Isaac dozing in his chair.

Hunter slapped his hand down on the desk near the man, the sound a loud pop not unlike a gunshot.

Isaac jumped and then mumbled something about needing to sample the strain before he opened his eyes. His expression changed to fear the moment he saw Hunter, and the storage unit manager jumped to attention. "Agent O'Neil." Rubbing sleep out of his bloodshot eyes, Isaac chuckled nervously. "Dreams." He cleared his throat and asked in a voice he'd clearly been practicing, considering it bordered on professional, "How can I help you?"

"Has anyone come through here in the last few hours?"

"Yeah. Some old lady who told me way too much about her bunions." Isaac shuddered. "And then some guy with a sourpuss face came in a minute later. I figured she'd caught him in the parking lot and treated him to the same story."

Cookie and Hunter glanced at each other, confirming they both thought it had to be Andy. "Thanks," Cookie said.

Isaac buzzed them in and she and Hunter took off toward Lydia's storage unit.

The moment they turned the corner they both pulled their weapons and walked slowly, keeping their movements as quiet as possible.

When they got to unit thirteen, they found the padlock they'd put on it had been cut open, but the door was down. Hunter crouched to grab the handle of the door and counted to three with just his fingers so Cookie'd be ready for whatever—or whoever—they might find.

The door thundered open to reveal Andy's angry glare. "You!" he screamed. His eyes were wild, and he gestured toward the freezer with the gun in his hand. "Where is she? What have you done with Lydia?"

Cookie and Hunter stood with their guns trained on Andy as Cookie realized Andy was not in his right mind. She spoke in a steady voice. "We needed the ME to examine her, Andy. She's at the—in his office. That's what happens in a murder investigation."

"You had no right." He waved the gun in the air as he spoke. "She was *mine.*" He slammed the pistol against his chest as if he were going to shoot himself in the heart, and every one of Cookie's muscles tensed in high alert.

"We were soulmates. Do you have any idea how rare that is?" His chest rose as he took a deep breath. "I'm never going to find another."

"Andy," Hunter said. "We can sort this out, but you need to put the gun down." Andy glanced at the weapon in his hand as if he didn't know how it got there. "That's it," Hunter continued. "Slow and steady, put it on the floor."

"I—" Andy shook his head and took another deep breath as the fight left him. He stuck the gun in the back of his pants. Tears streamed down his cheeks now as he spoke. "I'm not going to use it."

"I'd feel better if you put it on the floor, Andy," Hunter said, keeping his voice clear and void of any emotion.

Andy ignored him and looked at Cookie. "Have you ever loved someone so much you can't think of anything else? That the smell of their shampoo or the sound of their voice makes you smile? That when they're not with you, you can't wait to be together again?"

Cookie thought about the overwhelming passion one can feel when they first fall in love. Like the way Dylan sneaked into her thoughts throughout the day, and the way just the sight of him made her insides heat up with the glow of her emotions. She did love the way he smelled like the salty breeze that carried across the island mixed with a little bit of pine and old-fashioned soap.

Her heart skipped a beat as she wondered when Dylan would forgive her so they could be together again.

She smiled at the distraught man. "I do, Andy. It's wonderful." She lowered her gun to put him at ease, knowing Hunter would have her back. "And it's painful when it goes away, but when it does we have to find a way to move on." She took a step forward.

He nodded at her. "It didn't go away for me and Lydia." His expression turned to one of agitation again. "She just—" He let out a huff of air as his mood turned angry, and Cookie stopped in place. "Marriage is just a stupid piece of paper, but no." Andy's voice got hard. "Lydia couldn't leave him. Said it was a promise she made for life."

"That's tough, man," Hunter interjected. "What did you do?"

"What do you think I did?" Andy swept his arm around the room. "I told her I needed to see her one last time. I did this place up nice. You know? Champagne, candles, the works. She needed to see *we* were the real deal." He walked over to the dresser and yanked open a drawer to pull out a lacy bra. He glared at Cookie. "Do you know how much this stuff costs?"

"It's lovely," she said. "And that looks expensive. You have very good taste."

Andy tossed the lingerie on the bed and it landed with a soft *whoosh*. "It wasn't good enough for *Lydia*. She still said no." As if someone hit a switch, the man's mood flipped back to sadness, and Andy's voice cracked when he said, "So that's when I—I—" He lowered himself to sit on the bed and held his head in his hands. "Oh, god," he whimpered.

Cookie moved to sit beside Andy. The man was clearly not stable, and while a confession was important, she was more concerned that he still had his pistol. She said, "I'm going to take the gun now. Okay?" Andy nodded, and he reached back to remove the weapon from his pants. He cradled it in his hands as Cookie asked, "What happened, Andy?"

He looked at Cookie through a watery veil. "I didn't mean to. I just got so mad when Lydia wouldn't see reason." He broke out in a sob.

Hunter moved to crouch before Andy, putting his hand on the gun. But Andy clutched at the weapon, refusing to let go. "I get it," Hunter said. He didn't fight with Andy, but clicked the safety into place so that the pistol was one more step away from being dangerous. "Anger can take over and make you do things you didn't mean to do."

"Yes." Andy stared at Hunter for a moment then grabbed the bra that had been tossed on the bed earlier and handed it to Cookie. "Do you mind? It should go back with the others."

Cookie frowned. This apprehension was taking it's own sweet time. But she knew patience was key with suspects like Andy, so she took the lingerie from him and stood up to put it back in the drawer. As she walked over to the dresser, Andy said, "Anger can make me—" A loud thud made Cookie whip around to see Hunter crumple to the floor just as a shot rang out. The thunderous noise in such close quarters momentarily deafened her and she saw Andy mouth the word *kill*. Cookie grabbed her gun, but Andy got another shot off first, shattering the lamp sitting on the dresser behind her.

"Crap!" Cookie shot back but Andy was already in the storage facility's hallway. She raced over to the exit, but more gunshots rang out, keeping her from leaving unit thirteen.

Cookie's first instinct was to run after Andy once he cleared the corner, but her heart stopped with fear as she thought about Hunter on the floor, and Andy mouthing the word *kill* flashed in her mind. She turned to see about her former partner. "Hunter!" she yelled as she dropped to her knees to check on him.

Blood seemed to be everywhere as she felt for a pulse and realized he was still breathing. She took a breath of her own as Hunter blinked, pressing the palm of his hand to the minor head wound that was bleeding down his face. He let out a string of obscenities as he jumped to his feet.

"We're not letting that bastard get away!" he cried and took off running with Cookie at his heels.

21.

WHEN COOKIE AND Hunter got outside, they caught a glimpse of Andy before he turned onto Main Street. Their feet pounded loudly on the pavement as the two of them raced after Lydia's killer, but when they reached the corner Andy was nowhere to be seen. Cookie quickly scanned the area and her attention focused on the nearest business—the Salty Dog. "There!" she called, pointing at the entrance.

Cookie was breathless when she and Hunter entered the restaurant. Lowering their guns to be less conspicuous, they both scanned the dining room. Hunter's voice was low when he said, "Found him. Three o'clock."

Craning her neck to glance around one of the patrons, Cookie looked in the direction Hunter indicated to see Andy was slouched down in a booth trying to hide behind a menu. "Let's go crash his party," she said.

As they walked over to the table, Cookie was glad to note the restaurant wasn't very full. The last thing they needed were customers getting caught in the middle of a likely showdown. But as it turned out, customers weren't who she needed to worry about. Before they could reach the table, Daisy, the daughter of Larry Harris who was the owner of the Salty Dog, walked up to the booth where Andy was sitting.

In a split second, Andy was up and grabbed Daisy in a chokehold as he pressed a gun against her temple.

Cookie and Hunter reflexively lifted their guns as some other woman screamed. Silverware clattered on plates as the few customers jumped up from their tables to run for the door.

"Come any closer and she dies!" Andy yelled.

"Whoa," Hunter said as he and Cookie held their ground. "Nobody is dying here today, Andy. This isn't as bad as you think. From what I saw earlier and what you told us, this sounds like a case of mental distress. Isn't that right, Cookie?"

"Sure," Cookie said. She pulled out all the stops to talk Andy down and said, "Lydia really messed you up when she led you on, Andy. It was so unfair. Anyone could snap in that situation. Hunter's right. I'd push for temporary insanity if I were you."

Tightening his hold on Daisy, Andy averted his gaze and muttered something to himself about how Lydia had pushed him to do what he did.

Out of the corner of her eye, Cookie noticed the kitchen door was open a crack. She glanced over and it opened a sliver more, revealing Dylan, who winked at her. Daisy let out a whimper, making Cookie return her attention to the girl and Andy. She thought about the mess they'd seen in Andy's apartment and the shrine he'd left in the storage unit that made them believe he'd had trouble getting over losing Lydia. She said, "I'm sure you can provide plenty of evidence to show you weren't in your right mind, Andy. Don't you agree, Hunter?"

"Definitely," her former partner said.

Andy's frantic gaze shifted rapidly between Hunter and Cookie, and Cookie focused on Andy's eyes instead of Dylan, who was now slowly sneaking up behind the crazed murderer. She was sure that Hunter was doing his best to keep Andy's attention too.

"Heck," Hunter said, "Cookie and I can probably testify that you're still not in a sound mental state based on what we've witnessed so far."

Dylan was right behind Andy now, but Cookie didn't dare take her eyes off the man as she said, "That's right." She barely had the words out before they heard a loud crack followed by the thud of Andy's body hitting the ground.

"Oh!" Daisy cried, stumbling away and clutching at her throat. She quickly regained her footing, turned to Dylan, and threw herself in his arms.

Dylan grinned at Cookie over the top of Daisy's head and waved the frying pan with pride. "Cast iron'll do it every time."

As Hunter stepped forward to restrain Andy's limp wrists with a zip tie, Cookie smiled back at Dylan. That is until she noticed he had snaked his arm around Daisy's waist and had turned his attention to the pretty redhead who was clutching at him like she was drowning.

"You saved me!" Daisy gushed, smiling up at him.

Cookie understood how the woman felt. A cold metal gun against your temple was definitely cause for an emotional outburst when it was over. She might have even been okay with Dylan holding Daisy, his former high school flame, for comfort as well. But he went too far when he leaned down, giving her a tender kiss on the top of her head.

As if they were more than just friends. As if he still cared for Daisy. As if those years since high school had just disappeared in an instant. As if…

The old green-eyed monster of jealousy filled Cookie's mind with a rage like no other. And she suddenly understood exactly what Andy had been feeling when he strangled Lydia. But Cookie was not a killer, and she tamped down her anger as she pulled out her cell phone to contact Sheriff Watkins. She turned her attention to Hunter. "I'll get the coast guard to transport Andy to the mainland."

"And Swan," Hunter said.

"Right." Cookie said. They still had a dead deputy on their hands. And there was the matter of Rain moving Swan's body as well. She sighed. "Let's take Andy over to Swan's office," she added before Sherriff Watkins picked up her phone.

After the coast guard pickup was arranged, Cookie

and Hunter made their way out of the restaurant with a disoriented but conscious Andy held between them. When they got to the street, Cookie noticed Dylan had followed along. He stepped beside her and she blurted out, "We've got this. You might want to go back inside, though. Daisy could probably use more of your *help*."

Dylan raised his eyebrows at her as a smile played on his lips. "Perhaps I should."

Hunter cleared his throat. "We'll need your statement first."

Darn it. Cookie hadn't thought about that. Of course if she'd thought at all, she wouldn't have suggested Dylan comfort Daisy either. None of them spoke as they walked to the police station.

When they got there, Hunter suggested Andy be put in the back room to wait while they dealt with Swan. After they secured him, Cookie, Hunter and Dylan went to Swan's glass office. Hunter had made sure to draw the blinds before they left so that no unsuspecting person would walk into the station and notice Swan while they were hunting Andy.

Cookie turned to Dylan before they unlocked Swan's door. "There's something you should know about Swan's uh—condition."

"A little under the weather again?" he asked.

"Sort of," she said as she inserted the key they'd swiped from him earlier.

Hunter chuckled. "More like he suffered a *Rain* storm."

"It was not because of Rain," Cookie said defiantly as they stepped into the office where the very dead body of Swan was slumped in his oversized chair.

"Whoa," Dylan said. "What happened?"

Cookie answered as she noticed Hunter's body shaking with silent laughter. "Probably a heart attack, which my mother thinks was brought on by her striptease."

"She was stripping for him here?" Dylan asked, his question completely matter-of-fact as if nothing Rain did surprised him.

"No. He was at the inn," Cookie said with a sigh.

Hunter couldn't help himself and burst out laughing. When Cookie glared at him, he held up his hand and did his best to control it. "I'm sorry. But this is funny." Another small burst of laughter escaped before he continued, "Dylan, Rain decided that she killed him with her—ahem—dance. And since she didn't want to get caught, she and Winter decided to drive him to the station and make it look like it happened here."

Dylan's eyebrows shot up. "Those two women moved a dead body?"

Hunter was laughing uncontrollably now, and he wiped a tear from his eye as he croaked out, "In my car. And when we saw them, Swan's face was in—in Rain's—"

Dylan started laughing too. Apparently he'd connected the dots. When Cookie tried to get him to stop with her best laser-beam glare, he said, "C'mon, Cookie. You have to admit, this is funny. This kind of thing only happens to Rain."

Laughter *is* contagious. And no matter how hard Cookie tried to maintain her composure she found herself laughing too. When she stopped she said, "Fine. It's funny. But what are we going to do now?"

22.

C OOKIE, HUNTER AND Dylan all stared at the dead body of Deputy Swan for a moment before Hunter said, "You can't just move a dead body without suspicion."

"I know," Cookie said.

"But we all know Rain would never kill a man," Dylan added.

"Intentionally," Hunter said, snorting out a bit of leftover laughter.

"And it could have happened here," Cookie said.

"True," Hunter agreed. "Or maybe Rain and Winter decided to help us out by bringing the body here. Waiting at the inn for the ME to arrive would have taken hours since the ferry's out of commission."

"Right," Cookie said, nodding at his line of reasoning. "And a dead body is bad for inn business."

"Very bad," Dylan said. "For the island too. Most local businesses depend on tourism."

"Exactly," Hunter said. "It was a PR decision even

Swan could have gotten behind."

"Then it's settled," Cookie said. "We'll tell Watkins that it happened at the inn and the body was transported here for pick up."

Dylan began to laugh again. "They really—"

"They did," Hunter confirmed before he started laughing again too.

Cookie rolled her eyes at them and left the office to check on Andy. She did see the humor, but when it was your mother who was the brunt of a joke, it wasn't always easy to laugh. Once she made sure Andy was still restrained, she pulled out her phone and walked down the hall to the vending machines to make a call and check on Rain.

"Cookie! I'm so glad you called. Did you get the perp?"

Cookie chuckled. Rain's terminology was definitely improving. "We got him, Mom. How are you holding up?"

Rain let out a sigh that was heavy with the weight of her guilt. "I can't believe I killed Deputy Swan."

"You didn't," Cookie reassured her. "His death was due to a long history of overindulging. My guess is Jared is going to tell us he was a walking time bomb."

"One with a hair trigger I snapped," Rain said, her voice thick as if she was holding back a sob. "I've always known I had a dangerous effect on men, but—"

"But nothing," Cookie interjected. "Mother. Really. You are not why Swan died. Okay?"

"If you say so dear." Rain's voice didn't come across as someone who was convinced, though.

"I do," Cookie said sternly before she decided to change the subject to something lighter. "Do you still have plans to go out with Hale tonight?"

"I certainly do," Rain answered in a suggestive tone. "First I'm going to—"

"Mom," Cookie said in an effort to cut her mother off before she heard things that might scar her psyche for life. "I've got to get back to work, but I'll be home soon."

"Oh goodie! You're going to make your date after all."

Cookie considered the way Dylan had been acting as if nothing was wrong while they determined what to do about Swan, and it occurred to her that perhaps her little display of jealousy over Daisy might have been a good thing after all. It also occurred to her that Dylan didn't reply to the phone call she'd made earlier about dropping by to see him once she and Hunter had apprehended Andy. She'd have to see about that. And the fact that Dylan had been hanging out at the Salty Dog where Daisy worked.

"Perhaps I will," Cookie said to her mother and then returned to Swan's office to talk to Dylan.

But when she got there, Dylan was gone. Cookie frowned at Hunter, who said, "I took his statement and there wasn't any reason he needed to stick around."

"Oh." Cookie was scowling now, because she was even more confused about where she stood with Dylan.

Did they have a date or not?

"What's wrong?" Hunter asked.

She shook her head. Involving Hunter was not something she was going to do. No. She needed to make clear boundaries between Dylan and Hunter. "Nothing," Cookie lied. "I was thinking about my mother."

Hunter smiled with laughter in his eyes, but sobered quickly when she didn't return his amusement. "Right. Watkins should be here any minute, and then we can return to the inn and check on her."

Cookie nodded as her stomach growled. She hadn't taken the time to eat lunch and decided the time spent waiting could be filled by a snack from the vending machine.

Watkins arrived just as Cookie was finishing her candy bar. The woman pushed her way in with a team to deal with Andy and one to deal with Swan. As her officers got to work, Sheriff Watkins spoke to them. "Agent O'Neil, Ms. James," she said. "Thank you for your hard work on this." Hunter and Cookie nodded at Sherriff Watkins, and the woman sighed before she continued. "It's a darn shame about Deputy Swan. I'm told heart attacks are a quick way to go though. At least he didn't suffer at the end of his life."

"No," Hunter said. "I believe he was enjoying himself right up until the end." Cookie jammed her elbow into his side before he could break out in laughter.

"I'll find you a replacement deputy as soon as possible," the sheriff said.

Cookie didn't want to be rude or anger the sheriff, but she was concerned about who might come to fill the position as deputy on her island. Considering she'd resigned herself to the fact that trouble seemed to happen here, Cookie wanted to be sure Swan's replacement would be more competent than he had been. And this was her chance to have input. "You know," she said, "It's going to take a special kind of person to be the new deputy. Not only will this law enforcement officer have to deal with the small town politics on Secret Seal Isle, but—" she glanced over at the two men escorting Andy out of the building. She thought about how most of the businesses on this island relied on summer visitors and the money they spent for income. "Solid experience with the law is important. We are a tourist destination, after all."

"Yes. This island is getting a reputation for being rather busy when it comes to crime. I believe you're right in expressing concern," Watkins said. "I'll take that into consideration."

"Thank you."

"One more matter before I go," the sheriff said. "Could you step in as acting deputy for the time being?"

"Oh," Cookie said as she glanced at Hunter. She was certainly more than qualified as a former FBI agent to be the deputy on a small island. And it was very likely there wouldn't be anything for her to do in the next few days, but she was hesitant just the same. Only, there really wasn't anyone else to do it, so she said, "Of course." And out of respect for her new superior she added, "I'd be honored."

The wheels of a stretcher rumbled as it approached them, and as Cookie watched it roll by with Swan, sadness washed over her. The deputy may not have been the most competent man when it came to the law, but he wasn't a bad person, despite his obvious drinking problem. And death did come too soon for him. She was sure he would be missed. While she knew he didn't have relatives living on the island, Cookie recalled that Swan had family on the mainland and assumed that would be where the deputy's funeral would be held.

Cookie knew the island residents would need some closure too so she asked, "Shall I make arrangements for a memorial service here?"

The sheriff smiled at her. "That's a lovely offer. I'll pass it along to Deputy Swan's family." She shook Cookie's hand in appreciation. "Thank you, Deputy James."

"You're welcome," she said before the sheriff walked away.

The moment Watkins was gone, Cookie looked at Hunter, and when he frowned at her she held up a hand. "Don't say it. The woman didn't exactly leave me a choice."

Hunter smiled. "It was the right thing to do. *Deputy*."

Cookie sighed. She'd moved to Secret Seal Isle with her mother. They'd changed their names and become innkeepers to hide from a mob boss who wanted Cookie dead. Things here were supposed to be peaceful, even boring, perhaps. And Cookie had planned to welcome small town life with open arms.

Instead, weeks after Cookie and Rain arrived, a dead body floated up to her dock and life on Secret Seal Isle changed forever. No matter how hard she tried to lead a simple life, Cookie couldn't seem to escape her career in law enforcement.

The metal of her deputy star was smooth under Cookie's fingers when she rubbed it, and she realized it had just taken on a new meaning. "It's just for a few days," she said to Hunter. "And then I'll go back to being nothing more than an innkeeper on a small island in Maine." But Cookie wasn't sure who she was trying to convince—herself or Agent O'Neil.

23.

As Cookie and Hunter approached the inn on foot, Cookie noticed the twinkling lights that adorned the old Victorian building. Set in the snow-covered landscape, the place appeared to be a quaint establishment full of charm, laughter and warmth. She knew the moment they entered the door that delicious smells ranging from a savory roast to fresh-baked cookies would greet them. No matter what was going down in Rain's life, she could always be found cooking up a storm in their kitchen.

Cookie was proud of what she and her mother had created. In fact, they'd both settled in so well that they'd each found love interests too. But when Cookie walked through the front door, it was no longer clear Rain was so lucky in the romance department.

"I can't believe you'd do this to me," Hale, Rain's boyfriend about twenty years her junior, said, clutching his heart as if she'd just stabbed him. Rain stared up at the tall, slim man and reached up to brush a lock of his dark curly hair out of his wounded eyes. But Hale jerked back. "No. I'm not going to let you charm me into forgiving you. Not this time."

Hunter gently closed the door behind them, but the sound was enough to get both Rain and Hale's attention. Rain's worried gaze landed on Cookie and she ran over to her daughter. "Cookie, please, tell Hale I wasn't dating Swan."

Cookie glanced between the two of them, taking in Hale's angry expression and her mother's desperate one. "I don't think I should get in the middle of—"

"Sweetie, please!" Rain took her daughter by the hand and pulled her in deeper into the house. "I tried to explain why Deputy Swan's face was in my cleavage, but Hale doesn't believe me."

A small gasp came from the sitting area to the left of the entry hall. Cookie glanced over to see an older couple perched on the edge of the couch, munching on a bowl of popcorn, watching the fight as if they'd purchased tickets for a 3D feature film.

"Face in the cleavage sounds pretty damning to me," the woman said to her husband. "There's just no answering for that. It's not like some stranger is going to be checking the girls for moles, if you know what I mean."

The old man sitting next to her sighed. "Now that's a job I'd sign up for."

His wife swatted him. "If you'd gone to medical school like my daddy told you to instead of joining the army, you might've had a chance. It's your own fault." The woman with bottle-red hair glanced down at her ample chest, gave an approving nod and cupped her own breasts. "Though I dare say you didn't have to suffer much having access to these glorious tatas for the last forty years."

Her husband's gaze shifted to her cleavage now spilling out of her low cut sweater. He sucked in a sharp breath and practically drooled. "When you're right, Millie, you're right. Now ditch that popcorn. We're headed upstairs to…" The old man glanced at everyone now staring at them and smiled. "We need to check for moles." His attention narrowed in on Hale and Rain. "Let us know how this spat turns out between you two love birds… only save it for later. Much later."

His wife giggled as she let him haul her upstairs.

"At least someone is getting some on this Valentine's Day," said Scarlett from the open door of Cookie and Rain's office. She was dressed in black yoga pants and a soft red sweater, and her hair was piled artfully on her head, secured with two pencils. Her effortless elegance would've irritated Cookie, if she hadn't loved her so much.

Hale let out a disgusted snort as he turned and reached for the front door. "This entire conversation is pointless. I know what I saw. I should just go."

"Hale!" Rain cried. "Swan was—"

The door slammed behind Hale, and all that could be heard was the sound of his boots clattering on the front steps as he took off for his delivery truck parked at the end of the circular drive.

"—dead," Rain finished, her tone sad and dejected. Tears welled in her big wide eyes. "Now I've done it. I've gone and lost the best man I've ever had all because I accidentally killed a man." She sniffled. "And when I say best, I really mean *best*. The things that man can do—"

"Mom, you didn't kill Swan," Cookie insisted again. "He died of natural causes."

Hunter cleared his throat. "I think maybe I'll head on up and get a shower."

"Good plan," Cookie said and moved to put an arm around her mother as Hunter escaped up the stairs. "I'm sure not all hope is lost, Mom."

"It doesn't matter. I'll probably be in jail soon anyway." She stared at the floor, her voice dejected. When she glanced back up, her expression was mournful. "Winter told me moving Swan was a bad idea. But then we came up with that plan, and how was I to know a dead man was going to feel me up?"

"You're not going to jail," Cookie said, squeezing her mother's hand. "Hunter has already explained to Watkins that we had the body moved to Swan's office until the Coast Guard could come for him since the ferry wasn't operating. It was a logistical discussion."

Rain's eyes widened then narrowed with mischief. "Agent Hunter O'Neill told the sheriff that?"

"Yes. You can thank him later."

"Don't worry. I plan on it." Rain pumped her

eyebrows, but then worry flashed in her eyes again and all her amusement vanished. "None of that changes the fact that Hale just stormed out of here."

Cookie led Rain over to the couch. "He just needs to cool down a little. Then you can explain… uh, well, you can tell him you were just helping with Winter's case. I'd leave out the part about Swan already being dead, though."

"Why?" Rain asked, wiping her eyes. "Shouldn't I just be honest with him? You know I can't keep a secret like that for long. Especially if I bring him some of those special brownies he likes so much." Her eyes lit up. "Yes, that will definitely help. Maybe caramel and chocolate chip brownies." Rain turned and moved quickly toward the kitchen. "I'll have to hurry if I'm going to take them to him tonight."

"Mother!" Cookie called, exasperated.

Scarlett laughed and walked over to Cookie, linking arms with her friend. "Come on. Let's go help her make her brownies."

"Help her?" Cookie asked, raising an eyebrow.

Scarlett shrugged one shoulder. "She's just needs a little support. She did get groped by a dead guy."

Cookie snorted out a huff of laughter. "That is never going to get old."

"Then her boyfriend left in a huff on Valentine's Day," Scarlett continued. "She's had a rough one."

Who hasn't? Cookie thought as she pulled out her phone, checking once again for messages from Dylan.

Nothing. She bit back a frown and followed Scarlett into the kitchen where her mother was standing at the top of a four-foot ladder, leaning over to grab something from the far right shelf.

"Rain!" Scarlett ran over and raised her hands in the air as if that would save the older woman from toppling head first off the rickety contraption.

"I'm fine. Just need to grab my stash." She stretched a little farther and wrapped her fingers around an old tin container that had *Flower Power* and a daisy stamped on the front.

"I did not need to know where she keeps her happy herbs," Cookie mumbled.

"Please. Like it was so hard to figure out." Rain climbed down from the ladder and took her place at the butcher block island, all the brownie ingredients spread out before her. "Do you think brownies are good enough? Maybe I should make him my special psyche-delic mushrooms instead. Herb crusted, lobster stuffed mushrooms. The last time I made those he kept me up for hours. With that man's flexibility, imagination, and stamina—"

"No mushrooms," Scarlett said as Cookie closed her eyes and tried to shake the disturbing images of her mother and Hale from her mind. "The brownies will be orgasmic enough."

"True. He gets the same look on his face when he dives into one of these babies as he does when he's frosting my muffin."

Cookie groaned and started to back up, intending to ditch the conversation. She didn't really need to be here for this, did she?

"Stop being such a prude," Scarlett gently admonished. "It's not like you haven't caught her in the act enough times. It's no secret your mom enjoys her male company."

"But I don't need to hear about it on a daily basis," Cookie insisted.

"Here." Scarlett grabbed a large chocolate chip cookie off a nearby tray and handed it over. "Eat this. It'll help."

Cookie eyed the treat and narrowed her eyes at her mother. "Is this safe? No special herbs or other additives?"

"Of course it is, sweetie," Rain said, rolling her eyes. "I don't leave the good stuff out where just anyone can get to it."

"Of course not. What was I thinking?" Cookie bit into the chocolate-filled dessert and moaned in pleasure.

"If you did more of that, I bet you and Dylan would get through these little bumps in the road faster," her mother said with a sly wink.

"Like you and Hale?" Cookie asked, leaning against the counter with her arms crossed over her chest. "Looked to me like all the moaning you seem to be doing hasn't helped in that department."

Rain averted her gaze back to her brownie mixture and bit down on her lower lip. "I messed up really bad this time, didn't I?" She jammed the whisk into the metal bowl and beat furiously at the contents. "If he had his face in some dead woman's cleavage, I wouldn't be happy either."

"You'd forgive him once you knew the circumstances, though," Scarlett said as she dipped her finger into the bowl to sample some of the batter.

"Sure. But I'm easy-going." Rain passed a bag of caramels to Cookie. "Would you unwrap these for me?"

"Sure, Mom." Cookie stepped up to the butcher block island and went to work.

"Listen, Rain," Scarlett said, helping Cookie with the caramels. "Here's what you do. Get your brownies made. Then go get all dolled up. Wear his favorite lingerie—"

"He prefers my rhinestone-studded G-string," Rain clarified. "Says he likes knowing my kitty's dressed and ready to party."

Cookie popped a couple of caramels in her mouth just to distract herself.

Scarlett chuckled. "Okay, then put on his favorite outfit and a pair of sexy heels, then bring him the brownies and whatever else you make and tell him you two are having a bedroom picnic. Naked."

Rain's eyes lit up. "Oh, I can be the dessert after the dessert."

"Sure. And if he gives you any pushback, just take your dress off right there in the doorway." Scarlett winked. "That one works every time."

"Scarlett!" Cookie cried. "Do not tell my mother to

flash anyone in public."

"Oh, Cookie. Relax," Rain said. "It wouldn't be the first time."

"I *know*. Why do you think I'm telling her not to encourage you?"

Rain patted her daughter's hand. "Don't worry about a thing. Scarlett's right. All I need is a little seduction and I can fix this." Then she eyed Cookie for a moment. "Are you all right? You seem a little stressed. Want me to leave you some of my brownies?"

"She has a point, Cookie," Scarlett said. "You do look a little distraught."

"I'm fine. I just have a date to get ready for." At least she hoped she still had a date. Dylan hadn't called, but that wasn't going to stop her from showing up at his place. "I'm going to shower. *Do not* leave me any special brownies."

"Don't forget to shave your legs!" Rain called after her. "Or do a little gardening. You wouldn't want Dylan to get lost in the bushes."

Cookie couldn't help a small chuckle as she escaped upstairs, leaving her mother and best friend giggling like school girls in the kitchen.

24.

WRAPPED IN A thick terrycloth robe, Cookie stood in just her wool socks, staring at her closet. Four rejected outfits had been discarded on her bed, including the red dress she owned. Unfortunately while she could claim she had a red dress, it was hardly date material. It was better suited for… well, nothing Cookie could think of, which was why there was still a price tag attached to the garment with a high neckline and lack of tailoring. So now her only choices were jeans and some sort of top to hopefully show off her curves.

Too bad the sexiest thing she could find was a white button-down shirt that sported a spaghetti stain on the left side of the chest. For a brief moment she considered her mother's closet. But then she imagined the horrors she would find. "Gah! I really need to go shopping," she muttered to herself as she tossed the blouse on the bed with the other rejected clothes.

A light knock sounded on her door.

Cookie pulled her robe tightly closed, expecting her

visitor to be Hunter since his room was right across the hall. But when she opened the door, she found Scarlett leaning against the doorjamb, smiling at her. "Hey. What's up?"

Scarlett scanned her friend from head to toe and nodded as if she were confirming something to herself. "I came to save you from your sorry wardrobe." Her always-put-together friend suddenly produced a silky red dress that seemingly came from nowhere. "This is what you're wearing on your date."

Cookie stared at the slinky thing then shook her head. "No. No way am I going to fit into *that*."

Scarlett pushed past her into the room and stopped dead in her tracks when she saw the pile of clothes on Cookie's bed. "You've got to be kidding me. Were these the clothes you were considering wearing tonight?"

Cookie sighed. "It's awful, isn't it?"

"Girl, we need a shopping day, STAT."

Hadn't she just been thinking the same thing? If she took Scarlett with her, there was no doubt she'd end up with a number of respectable outfits. But would her credit card survive?

Scarlett grabbed a hanger and hung up the red dress she'd brought then moved over to the bed. She picked up a pair of dress pants and gave Cookie a look of despair. "These look like something you'd wear in a courtroom."

Cookie winced. "They are. I used to wear them when I was called to testify."

"Out." Scarlett tossed them to the floor and picked up the stained white shirt. She dropped it on the pants without comment. She made a very audible sound of disgust when she found Cookie's version of a red dress, and if it were easier to tear fabric, Cookie had no doubt Scarlett would have ripped the dress to shreds before she added it to the reject pile. After soundly labeling the four other dresses as blasts from the past, Scarlett grabbed her red dress, thrust it at Cookie and said, "Put it on. That's an order. No way am I letting you out of the house in anything else on Valentine's Day."

Knowing she wasn't going to win this fight, Cookie dropped her robe and quickly stepped into the dress. Scarlett stepped behind her and helped her get the zipper in place.

"I don't know," Cookie said, pressing a hand to her abdomen. "It's really clinging to everything."

"That's the point." Scarlett gently pulled Cookie over to the full-length mirror hanging on the back of the door. "Damn, girl. Look at you. This dress is hugging all the right curves." She licked her finger and pretended to touch Cookie's butt before she flinched back dramatically. Hot!"

"And showing enough cleavage to tempt a blind man," Cookie added as she shook her head at her best friend.

Scarlett grinned. "Dylan isn't going to know what hit him. I bet he tries to get you out of this this thing the minute you walk through his front door."

Cookie highly doubted that scenario, but she certainly hoped he'd get there sooner rather than later. And she had to admit, as she stared at herself in the mirror, if anything was going to help her cause, it was Scarlett's red dress. The thing made her look like she was straight off a pinup poster.

"Here." Scarlett moved behind her friend once more and with deft hands, she fixed Cookie's long auburn hair into a fancy twist that showed off her long neck. "Now we're talking. All you need are a pair of eff me heels and you'll be all set."

"Heels?" Cookie glanced at her fur-lined boots with longing. It was still February in Maine, after all.

Scarlett followed her gaze and shook her head. "No. Absolutely not. I forbid it. The heels are what you're wearing. I'll even go out and warm up the inn's new truck before you go." Now that the inn was busier, Rain had insisted they get a vehicle for carting groceries and supplies to the inn from the ferry.

Cookie took one last look at her boots then sighed in resignation. "Okay. But don't think this is a going to be a regular situation."

Scarlett chuckled. "I wouldn't dream of it."

After Cookie squeezed her feet into four-inch heels, she and Scarlett made their way down the two flights of stairs. By the time Cookie reached the last step, her toes were already screaming to be released from the torture devices.

"Stop grimacing," Scarlett said. "It makes you look

constipated."

"Gee thanks."

A low whistle came from across the room, and Cookie spun to find Hunter rising from his spot on the couch. He'd cleaned up and was wearing black wool pants, a midnight blue sweater, and a blazer.

"You look nice," Cookie said, giving him a warm smile. "Plans tonight?"

"I was hoping to entice my former partner." His appreciative gaze swept over her, and when she frowned he quickly added, "As friends I mean. After what happened this morning, I wasn't sure what your plans were, and I didn't want you to be on your own for Valentine's Day." He glanced at Scarlett. "I thought we could all go together, maybe."

"I'd love to," Scarlett said without hesitation. "But Cookie has plans. How about we go get a drink and stuff ourselves with lobster and crème brulee?"

Hunter turned his amused, dark gaze on Scarlett. "Crème brulee?"

"Definitely. Maybe some flourless chocolate cake too. If we don't have dates, we might as well indulge where we can."

"Sounds like a plan."

"Good." Scarlett turned to Cookie. "I'm going to go warm up that truck now. Give me about fifteen minutes."

"Thanks," Cookie said and smoothed the red dress, trying and failing to not fidget. She wasn't used to showing off so many assets, and definitely not when Hunter was around.

Scarlett grabbed the keys off the hook at the check-in desk and disappeared out the front door.

An uncomfortable silence fell between Hunter and Cookie, and after a moment Cookie moved to the desk and started rummaging around in the top drawer for the card she'd purchased for Dylan.

"Looking for this?" Hunter held up the small plastic bag that contained the two cards they'd grabbed at Andy's store earlier.

She tilted her head to the side, eyeing him. *What was he up to?* She crossed over to him and took the bag, finding the card she'd purchased for Dylan. "Where's the other one you forced me to buy?"

He chuckled. "I didn't *force* you to do anything. But since you asked, it's right there in the in-basket."

Cookie turned and glanced at the basket on the check-in desk, the one her mother took care of every morning. The red envelope stood out like a beacon, and Cookie was surprised she hadn't noticed it sooner. Familiar handwriting had Rain's name scrawled across the front. She picked up the envelope and turned it over, noting it wasn't sealed.

"You'll probably want to sign it," Hunter suggested.

"You had me get this for my mother?" she asked, astonished he'd thought of her.

He shrugged. "It seemed like something she might like."

Cookie grinned, her heart swelling with the knowledge that Hunter cared enough to think of Rain. "Thank you. That was really thoughtful."

"Open it up."

Her brow furrowed as she pulled the card out of the envelope. "What are you—oh!" The irritating music filled the room as Cookie stared down at the card, noting there were half a dozen messages scribbled inside. Every guest they'd had over the last few days had signed it along with Scarlett and Hunter. "She's going to love this."

Hunter's lips curved into a small smile. "She does a lot for everyone here. She deserves it."

Cookie quickly scribbled a message to her mother, stuffed the card back in the envelope, and dropped it back in the basket. Then she launched herself at Hunter, giving him a fierce hug. "You're the best, you know that Agent O'Neill?"

His arms wrapped around her and he held her close as he whispered, "Don't you forget it, Charlie. And if things go south with your handyman, you know where to find me."

Before she could say anything else, he released her and headed for the front door. But just as he reached for the handle, the door burst open and Winter strode inside with Blake right behind her. Hunter quickly backed up, making room for them.

"Blake! It's good to see you," Cookie said warmly, moving to shake his hand. But the man opened his arms wide and embraced her in a hug.

"I don't think I can thank you enough for all you've done over the last few days." He pulled back and added, "Winter told me how hard you and your partner worked."

"There's no need to thank us," Cookie said, a huge smile claiming her lips. "We're just happy the right man was apprehended."

"Thank you anyway," Blake said and turned to Hunter, holding his hand out.

Hunter clasped his hand. "I'm sort of surprised you made it back to the island tonight. Did the ferry open back up?"

"No," Winter interjected. "But I couldn't wait until tomorrow to see my man. Not after being separated like we were. I employed the help of a lobsterman who owed me a favor or two." She gave Cookie a sly smile. "He has a sweet tooth for the edibles Rain's been concocting."

"Sure," Cookie said, staring at the ceiling while Hunter snorted. She glanced over at him and wondered when he'd stopped caring about Rain and Winter's questionable activities. Not long ago, any talk of their side business and he'd ignore it completely, acting as if he hadn't heard a word. Being an FBI agent meant he was in a tricky spot if anyone found out he knew anything about illegal drugs. In that sense, Rain and Winter had been a huge thorn in his side.

"Anyway, I got him to go pick up Blake. We were on our way back to his house for our Valentine's Day reunion and wanted to stop by and thank you properly." She slipped her arm around Blake and ran a hand down his chest. "You have no idea how much what you did means to us."

"I'm pretty sure we get the idea," Cookie said as she moved past them and opened the front door. "And we really don't want to hold up the reunion. Why don't you two go on and we'll catch up over brunch in a few days."

Winter eyed Cookie, seemingly taking in her red dress for the first time since she'd arrived. "Oh, I see. Looks like someone has *hot* plans of their own."

Cookie's face heated up from the assumption.

"So cute. Look at her blush, Blake," Winter gushed. "Well, we don't want to keep you from your date with…" she glanced at Hunter and back to Cookie and raised both eyebrows in question.

"Oh! No." Cookie shook her head. "I'm on my way to Dylan's."

"Gotcha. Well, Hunter, Cookie, have a good evening. We'll see you in a few days or so after we emerge from the love nest."

Blake laughed at Winter and thanked them both again. Then they were gone, and Hunter and Cookie were alone… again.

"I should probably get going," Cookie said.

Hunter shoved his hands in his pockets and nodded. "Probably. You don't want to keep the boyfriend waiting."

"If he's waiting at all," Cookie said under her breath.

"I'm sure he is, Charlie. If he's not, he's an idiot."

She met his gaze, staring at him with love and friendship filling her heart. "You're a good man, Hunter. Thank you for always being here for me."

He reached out and took her hand gently in his. "I know things have been a little weird. It's been hard to accept another man taking the role I hoped would be mine one day. But you have to know all I want is for you to be happy. And if Dylan is the person who puts a smile on your face, then that's who you should be with."

Cookie squeezed his fingers and in a thick voice said, "You don't know what your words mean to me."

"I think I do," he said with that cocky half-smile he wore so often. "Just tell him if he hurts you, he's going to have the FBI breathing down his neck."

Cookie let out a huff of laugher. "I'm sure he knows."

The front door swung open and Scarlett walked back in. "Truck's ready." She glanced at Hunter and swept her gaze over him. "Well, damn, O'Neill, you're looking mighty fine tonight. How about that date?"

"Date?" he shot back.

She glanced at Cookie then back at Hunter. "Didn't he just ask me out on Valentine's Day?"

"Actually, I think it was the other way around," Cookie said. She knew there'd been something between them the other night. "You should go. Have dinner. Get out of this inn with someone other than me or Rain for a change."

Scarlett turned her attention to her friend, studying her. "Are you sure about that? I could stay home, be here just in case…"

"Oh no." Cookie raised her hands and started to back up toward the door. "I'm not going into my date with Dylan expecting it to go south. And I sure as heck don't want you sitting home by yourself while Mom and I are out on Valentine's Day. Let Hunter take you out and show you a good time. He's not so bad when he's on his best behavior."

"Hey, no one said anything about best behavior," Hunter interjected.

Scarlett scoffed. "If you aren't, I'll just kick you in the balls. Still want to take me out for dinner?"

He laughed and placed his hand on the small of her back. "Absolutely. I wouldn't know what to do with a woman who wasn't occasionally threatening my manhood."

Cookie chuckled. "That's true."

"Well then, it's settled," Scarlett said. "Let's get dinner. And I insist on dessert."

Cookie grabbed her coat and followed them outside. She watched them climb into Hunter's Mustang then hopped into the truck. The cab was all warm and toasty just as Scarlett had promised. She only hoped Dylan's reception would be the same.

25.

NERVES FLARED TO life in Cookie's gut as she put the work truck into gear. She took a deep breath and stepped on the gas. Five blocks later as she pulled to a stop in front of Dylan Creed's house, the butterflies in her belly were still fluttering to match the ticking of the engine. She turned the key and the rumble stopped. Dylan's porch was lit up and light flooded from the front bay window, bathing the snow in a soft yellow glow. Warm. Welcoming. Cozy. She hoped.

Dylan's slate blue craftsman-style home was in pristine condition. He'd inherited it from his grandfather and had painstakingly restored it over the years. His house was gorgeous, and besides the inn, it was her favorite place on the island.

Clutching her coat tightly around her, Cookie carefully made her way up the icy walkway. A gusty wind blew off the ocean, chilling her to the bone, and she shivered, praying she wasn't going to lose a toe or two to frostbite. She still couldn't believe she'd let Scarlett talk her into the four-inch stilettos. But if they did their job, it'd be worth every second of pain.

When she arrived on the porch, she took a deep breath and rang the bell. It took less than a minute for Dylan to come to the door, but it felt like a lifetime before he opened up and blinked in surprise.

Cookie did too. Because Dylan was in pair of dark gray suit slacks, a white dress shirt closed at the collar and an open jacket. Two blue neckties were in his hand. "Cookie. What are you doing here?"

Her heart sank as a wave of nausea came over her. Dylan had a date all right, but it mustn't be with Cookie. Tears filled her eyes as she realized how foolish she looked. "I… Ah—I just wanted to stop by and—" Dylan's expression turned to amusement, and the idea that he was laughing at her made anger begin to simmer in her veins. "Never mind," she snapped.

Cookie was about to turn and run as fast as she could in her stupid heels before Dylan reached out and grabbed her hand. "Get in here. I expected to pick you up, not the other way around."

"Oh," she said as she stepped into Dylan's warm house. "Ooohhhh." Cookie squeezed her eyes shut as she tugged her coat tightly around herself while a wave of embarrassment turned her face the shade of her dress.

To his credit, Dylan pretended not to notice and asked, "Which tie?"

Cookie opened her eyes, and without missing a beat she pointed to the one he was holding in his right hand.

"That one."

Dylan walked over to the mirror hanging above a small catchall table in the entryway and as he looped the tie together, he said, "I'd planned to take you to Blue Poisson, but since the ferry is closed, we have a reservation at the Salty Dog at seven. Since you're early we can sit at the bar for a drink or we can have one here." Since dining options on the island were limited the Salty Dog was known to spruce up the place with linens and candles for special occasions like Valentine's Day.

She looked over at the most comfortable leather couch she'd ever sat on and then the warm fireplace where she'd spent a few evenings cuddled next to Dylan, and suddenly she had no desire to go anywhere. "I think a drink here would be nice."

"Great. Let me take your coat, and I'll get us the champagne I have chilling." He walked behind her and helped her out of her jacket. Once she was free, Dylan stepped back and took in the sight of Cookie. "Wow. That's quite the dress."

Now she blushed in a good way. "Thanks. I borrowed it from Scarlett."

"Steal it." Dylan winked at her before he turned to go into the kitchen.

As he got the drinks, Cookie grabbed the remote for the gas fireplace, and it *whooshed* with flames when she turned it on. She placed herself on the couch, trying her best to sit in a way that was ladylike, even though she longed to kick off her shoes and tuck her feet under herself.

There was a time in her life when Cookie wished she were more like other woman who enjoyed dressing up and dining at the finest restaurants or frequenting the trendy nightspots. But living on an island where those options were limited, Cookie hadn't missed the nightlife of the city at all. While she did like to dress up once in a while, it was fast becoming clear that Cookie really was a comfortable-clothing kind of girl. She almost wished Dylan and she were getting take-out pizza and spending their evening talking and laughing in front of the fire.

When Dylan walked back into the room with two flutes and the champagne in an ice bucket, his smile pulled Cookie out of her thoughts. He said, "You look beautiful tonight."

"Thank you." She noticed the way Dylan made a suit appear as if he wore it every day. And he wore it well. It was tapered nicely down his torso, and she longed for a peek of what it did for his backside. "You look pretty amazing tonight, too."

"This old thing?" he quipped.

She laughed as he handed her a flute of champagne and sat next to her. He had a serious look on his face, and Cookie knew they both needed to clear the air. Before he could speak she went first. "Dylan, I'm sorry about my behavior over Daisy earlier." And since she was putting it all out there, she said, "And about the pushy way I came over tonight. As much as I hate to admit it,

I'm a little insecure."

"It's okay. I know how it looked, and I'm not always the best communicator. It's understandable you weren't sure about tonight. I'll try to do better with that." He gave her the once-over with his gaze. "And I like a woman who takes charge." Dylan chuckled and took a deep breath before slowly releasing it. "I wasn't exactly rational when I saw you with Hunter at breakfast this morning."

"It's okay." Cookie smiled as she repeated his words. "I know how it looked, and I'll try to be more sensitive to that in the future."

Dylan lifted his glass for a toast and Cookie did the same as he said, "To the only woman I want to spend Valentine's Day with. May there be many more."

"I'd like that." Their glasses clinked as they tapped them. "Very much," Cookie added before she took a sip of her drink. Bubbles danced on her tongue as she tasted the tart champagne and swallowed it down.

"What are the occupants of the inn up to tonight?" Dylan asked.

"Let's see. Well, Rain is on a date with Hale, and Scarlett and Hunter went out as well."

"Did they?" Dylan reached for her glass. "So you haven't got anyone to worry about tonight."

"No." She handed him her drink so he could set it on the coffee table.

"That makes you all mine until tomorrow morning," Dylan said, and when he leaned in for a kiss, Cookie met him. The faint taste of alcohol was on his lips, but as their tongues flitted and twined together the flavor was all Dylan, and she drank him in.

When they broke apart he placed a finger along the edge of her dress by her collarbone. Cookie shivered a little from his touch as he traced her neckline lower. "You wore a red dress."

She reached out, tucking her fingers under the lapel of his jacket. "And you wore a dress shirt I assume requires cuff links."

He lifted his arm to show her the cuff of his shirt. "It does."

Dylan gave her a sly look and then bent down to lift up one of her feet. He slipped off a shoe. "Stilettos. Nice," he said as he set it down and removed her other one.

Cookie reached forward and grabbed his tie with a mischievous smile of her own. "Blue tie to match your eyes." Cookie undid the knot to remove it. Because as sexy as Dylan looked in a suit, she preferred the casual version she was accustomed to better. The tie slithered off his neck as she tugged it. "Very nice," she said as she tossed it on the floor near her discarded heels. She had a feeling Dylan liked the real Cookie too.

Dylan stood and unfastened the top button on his shirt. He held out his hand. "Want to see what these pants do for my butt?"

Cookie nodded as her desire for more than a kiss ramped up, and she placed her hand in his. He led them to his bedroom, and when they got there Cookie gasped in surprise. The room was filled with dozens of candles, and on the bedside table was a vase of red roses. She walked over to smell them and noticed what looked like a take-out menu. "Uber Eats by Stone Harris?" she asked. She chuckled when she read the choices. It was basically a pared-down version of items from Stone's family's restaurant, the Salty Dog. She suspected he was the chef for this endeavor too, because the food options leaned toward the kinds of things a stoner would want to eat.

"Dylan Creed, you're not taking me out to dinner are you?"

He walked up behind her and leaned down to kiss the back of her neck. "That's up to you." She let out a small sigh, and Dylan said, "I'll take you wherever you want to go."

26.

COOKIE GAZED OUT at the crowd gathered for
Deputy Swan's memorial ceremony. While an
event of this sort was rare on Secret Seal Isle, causing a
number of people to come just for the chance to get out
and shake off some cabin fever, Cookie suspected there
were a vast majority of residents who missed the man and
really were here to mourn his loss.

Rain and Winter had done a lovely job decorating
the VFW hall in a tasteful way. They'd used just the
right amount of flowers while staying well within the
town's budget, which surprisingly had a line item for
memorial services. It helped that Andy DePaul's
stationery shop was having a going-out-of-business sale
where they'd picked up white and purple ribbon for next
to nothing. Cookie'd heard that one of Andy's nephews
had just returned from Switzerland after training to be a
chocolatier and planned to cut his teeth opening a sweet
shop for the summer.

Cookie noticed Winter fussing over the refreshment

table with Blake by her side. He said something to the woman that made her laugh, and they exchanged a brief kiss. Cookie's heart swelled with happiness for them. They were one of the reasons she loved being in law enforcement. Restoring order to everyday lives so that people could be happy was incredibly rewarding.

Cookie searched the room for her mother, a little nervous about what she'd find. It had been three days since her mother had found any trouble, and lately that was almost a record. She discovered Rain sitting next to one of Swan's relatives in the rows of chairs lined up in the hall. Hale was backstage helping Dylan with the lighting and sound, and Cookie imagined Rain was merely entertaining herself with conversation. Well, perhaps flirting was a better word for it, since Rain was talking with a very fit man who she was sure her mother was trying to console with more than words, judging by the way Rain was squeezing his bicep. Cookie almost wished Rain hadn't got past the idea that her charm could kill.

She smiled as she recalled the story surrounding Swan's death that'd had Hunter and Dylan laughing to the point of tears. And now that a few days had passed, she too had to admit it was funny.

"Cookie, hun, it's almost time," Scarlett said as she approached her with a camera around her neck. Scarlett had agreed to cover the memorial for the small town paper since the editor, writer, and photographer was on a cruise. Cookie smoothed out her suit jacket as she thought about her best friend, and her former partner, Hunter. While she hadn't gotten a lot of details about their date on Valentine's Day, Cookie had a feeling something more than friendship was brewing between two of the people she cared about most. And she approved.

Especially since her heart was firmly in camp Dylan. Or, more accurately, in Dylan Creed's hands. A tiny shiver of desire ran down her back as she recalled their evening staying in.

"Cookie?" Scarlett asked before she chuckled. "Briefs or boxers?"

"What?"

"I'm just asking which you just threw on the floor of your imaginary bedroom, because you sure as hell aren't here."

Cookie flushed. "That's not what I—oh never mind." She knew that no matter what she tried to tell Scarlett, the truth was her friend knew her well enough that it was a waste of time to lie. She took a deep breath and prepared herself to step on the stage and address the town on behalf of Deputy Swan.

That is until a thunderous sound, much like a storm, began. As it got louder, Cookie recognized the noise. *Was that a*—She glanced over at Dylan who was on the stage making sure the microphone was working. He frowned at her and they both mouthed the word *helicopter* at the same time. The building around them shuddered, and someone threw open the doors to reveal it was, in fact, a helicopter that had just landed on the street, smack dab in front of the VFW hall.

A man and a woman with television cameras hopped out first, followed by another guy in a police uniform. He held out his hand for a woman who stepped out in a navy blue skirt and jacket. The woman was short. She was also round. And something about her smile was familiar.

As the woman began to walk down the aisle between the rows of chairs toward Cookie, she smiled and waved to the seated crowd as if she was a queen or perhaps a very friendly bride. "Who in the world is that?" Scarlett asked in a loud whisper.

Dylan was now by Cookie's side and asked, "Is that—"

Cookie's jaw dropped when she noticed something very large and shimmery on the woman's jacket.

"Blue eye shadow she's wearing?" Scarlett asked as she shuddered. "That color is reserved for Cher and Ru Paul."

"Yes," Dylan said." But I was asking about the—"

"Super-sized deputy star?" Cookie finished for him.

"Yup," Dylan said.

"I think that's the new law in this town," Cookie said as the woman locked eyes with her. Cookie's heart sank. She tried really hard not to judge a book by its cover, but the fact this woman helicoptered into town for a memorial service screamed DRAMA LLAMA in capital letters. She tried to hold on to the hope that despite this woman's theatrical entrance that perhaps she was a competent officer of the law too.

"June Loon!" the woman sang, holding her hand out to Cookie in greeting. "It's a pleasure to meet you, Cookie James. I've heard so much about you." She gripped Cookie's fingers tightly and lowered her voice to a whisper as she petted the gold star pinned to her chest. "I'm the new deputy, and I've prepared your introduction for me."

June turned to the tall, thin officer next to her. "Zeke."

The man thrust a piece of paper into Cookie's hands, and she began to read it.

"Well, hello," June drawled as she spotted Hale on the stage staring at her in wonder. Or perhaps it was straight-up shock. "Come be a dear and help me up those stairs, would you?" she asked him.

There were two steps up to the stage. But June made them appear to be an entire flight with the way she latched onto Hale's arm with one hand and pawed at his chest with the other, all while taking her sweet time maneuvering up the steps.

When she got onto the stage, she didn't let go of Hale as she hooked her finger at Cookie and said, "I believe the natives are getting restless."

Hale made a move to disengage from June, but she tightened her grip on him, holding the man in place.

Cookie frowned at the woman. She wasn't about to be steamrolled by the new deputy in town. "They can hold on for a minute more." She gave June her best saccharine smile. "You've given them something to talk about while they wait."

June giggled. "I certainly have, haven't I?"

Cookie shook her head and began to read the prepared speech, but she didn't get past the part where June was born in a shanty on the island, at the top of an icy hill, in the middle of a cold night in January, without power, before Rain appeared at her side.

Rain had a vast range of emotions she displayed on a daily basis, but her current state was reserved for very special occasions. Cookie could count on one hand the number of times she'd witnessed it. As Rain plucked the dangly feather baubles she was wearing out of her earlobes and handed them over, Cookie realized Rain was spitting mad. "Hold my earrings, dear. This won't be pretty."

27.

J UST AS RAIN was about to launch herself at June for a good old-fashioned cat fight, Dylan snaked an arm around her waist and pulled her back. "Dial it down a notch, Rain. Hale has no interest in June, and the poor woman hasn't got any idea what she's stepped into."

"And that's why I need to show her." Rain thrashed as she growled out, "Lemme at her!" Dylan grunted as he struggled to keep her in check.

Scarlett, in her infinite wisdom and vast experience as a lawyer representing the shadier side of life, stepped in front of Rain and into her space. In a calm, but very stern voice Scarlett said, "You're Queen Bee in this town, Rain. And nobody is going to steal that crown from you. Not on my watch. Got it?"

At that point a small crowd had gathered around them, and Winter pressed a lollipop into Rain's hand as she whispered. "Suck on this, honey. It'll help."

Hale had finally escaped June's clutches and pushed his way into the circle. Rain glared at him. "Now, Sweet

Cheeks," he cooed. "You know I think you hung the sun." He held out his hand. "Come on, let's go sit down."

Rain stuck the lollipop in her mouth and sucked loudly before she reluctantly took Hale's hand, muttering, "I hung the moon." She turned to Cookie and Scarlett and said, "He's not that smart." And then Cookie knew Rain was okay, because her mother placed her hand on Hale's backside, winked, and added, "But you know I don't mind teaching them to read in the morning."

"Whew," Scarlett said. "One crisis averted."

"Now on to the next one." Cookie grabbed Scarlett's arm. "Come with me." She and Scarlett marched up to the stage where June, having apparently ignored Rain's outburst, was instructing Zeke on how to lower the microphone.

"June," Cookie said, paper rustling as she waved the speech. "I've just come up with a brilliant idea." She turned to her friend. "Scarlett writes for the Secret Seal Times, and she'd love to take this information and do an article about you." When June's brow knit with her displeasure, Cookie said, "You know how short peoples' attention spans are these days." She sighed dramatically. "Words go in one ear and out the other. But the written word…" She paused for effect. "Well, that's forever. I think your introduction to the town as their new deputy deserves it. Don't you?"

"Well, I don't know," June mused.

Cookie jumped in before the new deputy could begin to make a case for herself. "Besides, it's really Deputy Swan we're focusing on today. I'm sure you understand."

"Do I ever," June grumbled. "He was my big brother, and I'm here to give his eulogy."

Cookie and Scarlett looked at each other in shock. Cookie seized the moment, because she was thrilled not to give Swan's eulogy, and she stepped in front of the mic before June could object.

"Ladies and gentlemen!" Cookie called out. She waited for the crowd to settle down. "It's my pleasure to introduce to you June Loon. She's Deputy Swan's sister, and has come to help us pay our respects." She turned to June and said, "June," before she moved out of the way to let the woman take over. She went and sat in her seat in the first row between Dylan and Scarlett.

June's voice was shrill, and the sound system squawked as she began. "Good morning, everyone! Goodness, look at all of you. It's so nice to be home." She giggled. "Barney Johnson? Is that you? Almost didn't recognize that cue ball of yours. Such a pity, you really had a lion's mane in the day." As Barney's face turned red she moved on. "And Nancy Morris, my gosh." She chuckled. "I bet you won't be squeezing into that cheerleader uniform for our reunion now, will you?"

Nancy glared at her as June said, "Oh dear, I've gone off on a tangent, haven't I? Let's get to the business at hand." June yammered on about her vast achievements, and Cookie tuned her out. She was about to gossip with Scarlett when her friend said, "Ah, Cookie. Don't look now, but one of those cameras is from WCVB. That's Boston's news station."

Cookie's heart stopped, and ice filled her veins as she pictured the sneering face of mob boss, Vinny DeMasi. Once she'd put him away for life he sworn he'd kill Cookie for what she'd done. Because of the danger, she'd chosen to resign from her position at the bureau. She and her mother had moved to Secret Seal Isle to hide. How could she have been so careless? She'd gotten so used to her quiet life and feeling safe in her sleepy little town that she'd let her guard down. Heck, she'd forgotten she even had one. She croaked out, "Were they taping when I spoke?"

Scarlett nodded. "I'm pretty sure they were. You and Rain need to get out of here. *Now.*"

"But—" She glanced at Dylan and saw his brow was knit in confusion.

"Go!" Scarlett urged. "Dylan and I will take care of this."

The moment Cookie began to walk she clicked into agent mode, and she moved quickly to get to Rain. When the two of them first relocated to the island, Rain had suggested they have a secret hand signal for SOS. Cookie had agreed, mostly to humor her mother, but right now she wanted to kiss Rain for it. When Cookie got to the aisle where her mother was seated, she captured Rain's attention and lifted up her thumb and pinky to wiggle them in the surfer's traditional hang-ten gesture.

Rain immediately hopped up and squeezed her way

out as she said, "Bird in the oven. You can't leave those things unattended for long."

They rushed outside to the truck, and once Rain slammed her door, Cookie said, "Mom, I wasn't thinking. When I spoke before the town a few minutes ago, a Boston news camera captured it."

"Oh, honey." Rain reached over and placed her hand on Cookie's arm. "Do we need to run? I'm ready." Cookie marveled at her mother's ability to switch gears in an instant. But she'd always known when it came down to it, Rain could be trusted to do whatever was necessary for them to stay alive. Her mother added, "I just switched out the medicinals in my go bag yesterday. I made you a little goodie bag too, just in case."

Not once had Cookie partaken in any of Rain's goodies, but that never stopped her mother from making sure they were available to her daughter if the need arose. And honestly, medicinals sounded good to Cookie right about now. She half wished Rain had still been sucking on her lollipop so she could have some too, because that might take the edge off her panic. "We don't need to run yet," she said. "Scarlett and Dylan are going to try to get the tapes, and we may be fine."

"Dylan?" her mother asked.

Dylan. Cookie sighed. She'd known that eventually she'd have to fill in the blanks about her past to Dylan, but she'd hoped it would be in a manner that let him know she trusted him, not because she had no choice. She supposed now was as good a time as any, though, because the fact he was involved with Cookie on a romantic level put him in danger. Telling him everything was long past due.

When she pulled up to the inn, tears filled Cookie's eyes. She gazed at the quaint Victorian on the sea, shining in the late afternoon sun. The porch swing swayed in the wind, inviting her to go sit and savor a warm cup of cocoa as she enjoyed the sea air. It had become her oasis, and she knew Rain loved their home just as much. "What have I done, Mom?"

"Nothing we can't handle," Rain said with the confidence in her voice Cookie needed to hear. She knew that no matter where she and Rain might have to land, they'd have each other. They'd have Hunter and Scarlett too. But what they'd lose would be the friends they'd made on the island they both now called home. And… Cookie's heart felt as if Vinny DeMasi had it in his meaty fist and was squeezing as hard as he could. Because if they had to run, she'd have to leave Dylan behind.

"Right," she said in resigned voice. "Nothing we can't handle."

She could leave the inn forever.

She could leave Secret Seal Isle forever too.

But Dylan? Her heart ached, knowing she wouldn't recover if she lost him. And in that moment, she knew she had a choice to make if she wanted to be free from Vinny DeMasi: run, or fight for everything she had at the risk of endangering the people she loved.

THE END

Find out more about Lucy Quinn's latest release at
www.lucyquinnauthor.com

Secret Seal Isle Mysteries
A New Corpse in Town
Life in the Dead Lane
A Walk on the Dead Side
Any Way You Bury It
Death is in the Air
Signed, Sealed, Fatal, I'm Yours
Sweet Corpse of Mine
Knocking on Death's Door

Lucy Quinn is the brainchild of New York Times bestselling author Deanna Chase and USA Today bestselling author Violet Vaughn. Having met over a decade ago in a lampwork bead forum, the pair were first what they like to call "show wives" as they traveled the country together, selling their handmade glass beads. So when they both started writing fiction, it seemed only natural for the two friends to pair up with their hilarious laugh-out-loud cozy mysteries. At least they think so. Now they travel the country, meeting up in various cities to plan each new Lucy Quinn book while giggling madly at themselves and the ridiculous situations they force on their characters. They very much hope you enjoy them as much as they do.

Deanna Chase, is a native Californian, transplanted to the slower paced lifestyle of southeastern Louisiana. When she isn't writing, she is often goofing off with her husband in New Orleans, playing with her two shih tzu dogs, or making glass beads.

Violet Vaughn lives on an island off the coast of Maine where she spends most mornings in the woods with her dogs, summers at the ocean, and winters skiing in the mountains.